The Light at St. Silvan's

Endorsements

Powerful. Contemplative. Fun. *The Light at St. Sylvan's* delivers a delightful plot wrapped in lyric prose and stirs up inspiration like a true friend. What a treat! Congratulations to author Murray Pura for another page-turner.
—**Cathy Krafve**, author of T*he Well: The Art of Drawing Out Authentic Conversations* and host of *Fireside Talk Radio*

The Light at St. Silvans by Murray Pura is more than a romance, more than another Amish read. This is a work of insight and poetry and imagery that immerses you in a world of healing and friendship and love. Once started, you will not put the novel down.
—**Carol McClain** award-winning author of *A New York Yankee on Stinking Creek* and *Borrowed Lives*.

Murray Pura's masterpiece, *The Light at St. Silvan's*, is an illuminating delight. From the moment readers enter the mind of Amish widow Sara King, we are privy to her metamorphosis into becoming the writer, Lyyndenna Patrick—not quite ex-Amish, not quite "English." With beautiful prose that seeps into the soul, to kitschy dialog with the English, and her own fantastical internal dialog, we are taken on a bittersweet spiritual journey that is painfully honest and elegantly hopeful. Pura's artistry with words sculpts a story that is multi-dimensional and defies categorization.
—**Terri Gillespie**, award-winning author of *Making Eye Contact with God*, *The Hair Mavens* Series, and *Sweet Rivalry*.

Murray's storytelling shines in this new work, *The Light of St. Silvan's*. Sara's story of loss is universal, and told with a twist—she's left the safety of the Amish community to discover who she

is. I was drawn in and couldn't put the book down.
—**Jane S. Daley**, author *Because of Grace, A Mother's Journey from Grief to Hope*

What impressed me most in Murray Pura's story, *The Light at St. Silvan's*, was the thoroughness in which the author fleshed out his protagonist's crisis of lifestyle—not to be confused with crisis of faith. The raw and unpredictable power of the Atlantic Ocean served as an ideal metaphor for Lyyndenna's cold, lonely journey. Though the protagonist had an Amish background, her story could easily resonate with any of us.
—**Clarice G. James**, author, *Doubleheader, The Girl He Knew, Party of One, Manhattan Grace.*

The Light at St. Silvan's relies on the spiritual solitude of a historic lighthouse cottage to blend several budding stories into one marvelously crafted and satisfying tale. For Sara King, a fresh start requires a new name, a fascinating change in location, and an intense test of former beliefs. Her sense of discovery is contagious throughout her healing journey, and Murray Para captures it brilliantly.
—**Janet Morris Grimes**, author of *Solomon's Porch*

I was both delighted and surprised as I read each page of Murray Pura's new book, *The Light at St. Silvan's*. He captured my full attention and intrigued me to journey along with a contemporary young Amish woman. With every chapter, he successfully wove together her story of heartache from her past with her hope and determination to begin a new life. Grab a cup of your favorite coffee and enjoy reading Murray's excellent book.
—**Billie Fulton**, author of Selah Award-winning *Faith Is Not Silent* and newly released, *Just A Moment, Changes Life Forever.*

Author Murray Pura gently explores betrayal, heartbreak, forgiveness, love, and redemption. The companionable *The Light of St. Silvan's* assures that when pain overwhelms, the solitary path is through where you find that God is at work even in this.
—**PeggySue Wells** is the bestselling author of 29 books including Chasing Sunrise, Homeless for the Holidays, and The Ten Best Decisions A Single Mom Can Make.

The Light at St. Silvan's

Murray Pura

ELK LAKE PUBLISHING INC

PUBLISHING THE POSITIVE
Plymouth, Massachusetts

Copyright Notice

Cover and Interior Design: Derinda Babcock

Editor(s): Cristel Phelps, Deb Haggerty

PUBLISHED BY: Elk Lake Publishing, Inc., 35 Dogwood Drive, Plymouth, MA 02360, 2021

Library Cataloging Data

Names: Pura, Murray (Murray Pura)

The Light at St. Silvan's / Murray Pura

256 p. 23cm × 15cm (9in × 6 in.)

Identifiers: ISBN-13: 978-1-64949-158-9 (paperback) | 978-1-64949-159-6 (trade paperback) | 978-1-64949-160-2 (e-book)

Key Words: Amish/Mennonite, Self-Discovery, Romance, Coming of Age, Literature, Islands & Ocean, Spiritual

Library of Congress Control Number: 2021933788 Fiction

Dedication

But one man loved the pilgrim soul in you
And loved the sorrows of your changing face
William Butler Yeats, "When You Are Old"

Acknowledgments

I want to express my thanks to Deb Haggerty whose enthusiasm for this project ensured St. Silvan's saw the break of day in the best version possible. I also want to thank Cristel Phelps who, along with Deb, helped hone the manuscript, and to Derinda Babcock who brought the cover to life.

Part One (April to December)

Chapter One—Leaving and Becoming

Not that she did not wish to have friends--she loved to be around people. Not that she wanted to keep all her thoughts to herself--sharing her feelings with others, and listening to others share theirs with her, was an important part of her days and weeks. No, but just to be alone, by the sea, in the light, was a time to discover who she was, to know her soul in all its depth and intricacy and mystery. By the sea was a place to dream, to pray, to worship, perhaps even to dance where no one was watching except the gulls that swooped across a sky of blue or gray or gold. Here was a place only God knew, and here was where she came to know God.

A strange admission, Sara King thought to herself. After all, she had been raised Amish, baptized Amish, married Amish. She was an Amish woman. Sometimes she felt she was more Amish than she was American.

Where ocean met sky did not seem real. There was so much of everything--air, wind, water, space--it was as if all of heaven was over her head and in front of her eyes. Trying to take it in, she felt she had to become a new person because what she used to be could not hope to contain the half of what rushed over her senses. She reached out with her hands to hold it but it slipped through her fingers and into her heart, all of it. She became the sea. She became the air and the sky, became the long stretch of shore and all its sand and rocks. When a wave broke into a spray of light, it was her.

It had never been easy. No matter what the tourists thought about the Amish--theirs was not life under a lilac bloom. Amish life was not the way so many of those who wrote Amish stories said it was--one long romance with God, and with farming, horses, and the land under beautiful sunny skies. One long romance with your man. The life could be so wonderful, yes. But that way of life could be hard. Hard as hidden boulders striking a plow.

"I am being born," she whispered. But there was no pain. Not for her, not for her mother, and not for anyone else. There was only the release, the freedom, a delight that carried a child's innocence and a young girl's wonder at seeing beauty for the first time.

There had been one son. Sara was unable to conceive after that. Doctors were no help. Her husband blamed her. Why did he marry her? Why could she not give them a family like the Millers or Bylers or Hostetlers? When the boy had been killed in a farming accident at eight, her husband could not forgive God. Nor could he forgive himself. He could never forgive himself. Many tried to help. She could not deny that. So many in the Amish church tried to help them in their dark and terrible grief. But he took his life with rope in the barn. While she was in the house preparing their lunch. It was a cloudless April day. She thought of it as a perfect day, though her heart remained dark with the loss of her boy the month before. Perhaps the best day since the accident. She looked out the kitchen window at the farmyard while she peeled carrots. The barn was green and huge and silent, and her husband did not respond when she opened the window and called him to the table.

The light cut through mist and darkness and warned sailors about the rocks at St. Silvan's. It also guided them to port and to safety, no matter what sort of problems they were dealing with in their ships or what sort of storms they were attempting to weather. She often wished, as she stood on the upper deck of the lighthouse and watched its beam stretch over the waters, that the light could do the same for her. At such times she began to pray, and the prayer was nothing like church prayers at all. They came up from deep within her and were often as wild and rugged as the Atlantic itself. But they were her words, and they were from her heart, and somehow, she was aware God knew that and loved her for them. That love burned through any night that had descended on her and any storm or cloud that shrouded her soul.

Sara King never thought of herself as someone who might run. But her husband's suicide, falling so hard upon her son's death, after a marriage of bitter words from a man who could not accept her or love her as she was, caused everything to collapse. A year after the loss of her son and her husband, she left. She gave the farm to the bishop in a legal document he would not receive until after she was gone. Friends who had helped her work the farm that lonely year would take care of things while she was away. She told them it was only for a few days.

She had taken the train and the bus and finally an Uber. Then several ferries, including one that only sailed on Fridays until July and August when it made the trip once a day. Her bid on an old abandoned lightkeepers' cottage on St. Silvan's had been accepted. A realtor met her on the mainland in Gloucester. They did the paperwork and Sara was handed the keys.

"It's fine for summer," the realtor told her. "Of course, it's winterized too. Keepers lived there year-round. But it will need a bit of TLC."

"Thank you," Sara responded. "I'll take care of that."

"Oh, are you handy?"

"I am, yes."

"Are you a carpenter?"

"I am a farmer. One who didn't stay in the kitchen or laundry room."

"Will your family be joining you on St. Silvan's?"

"No, they will not."

Sara had boarded the first train dressed Amish but changed into jeans and a blue chamois shirt in a restroom in the car, tying her sand-colored hair back with a blue bandana. She took her battered navy backpack onto the ferries along with a sky-blue mountain bike she bought in Gloucester. A man on the first ferry told her everything matched her eyes. She surprised herself by her reply. "My eyes aren't yellow like my hair."

The smell of the sea overpowered her and broke through all her fear and doubt about what she was doing. The tar of the wharves, the gray planks, the roll of the ferries, the spray, the gulls, all were part of a magic kingdom that promised far more than what she had left behind. Yet she sang an Amish hymn to herself as the ferry approached the wharf at St. Silvan's. And said a prayer in High German out loud when she unlocked the door to her cottage and stepped inside after a ten-minute bike ride. Peace. An overwhelming sense of peace.

"Lived in but lived in well," she said, after one long glance.

She knew keepers and their families had lived in the cottage since 1705 and that the house had been improved upon a dozen times to add plumbing and wiring and new roofs. But because most of it was stone, it had withstood the test of time and storm without sinking. Furniture from the 1700s and 1800s had been removed to a museum in Gloucester. The description of the property had said most of what remained was from the 1930s and '40s, though the large oak desk was from 1912. She sat in one of the solid wooden chairs. There had been one room, then two, then three. When the light was automated in the 1970s, the government had turned the house into a writers' retreat—the only stipulations being occupants could stay no longer than three years, they had to write about the sea, and they had to have published something beforehand, however small or light.

After forty-five years, the government wanted the old cottage off their hands and listed it with the Gloucester realtor she had purchased it through. Since the lightkeeper's house was a heritage property, all sorts of do's and don'ts were involved, which was enough to scare off any number of potential buyers. On top of that, no more than two people be in residence. There had to be a family connection to the sea through fishing or the Coast Guard or the Navy. There had to be a writer of fiction, preferably sea fiction, somewhere in the lineage. The successful buyer had to agree to write a weekly blog about the island that was upbeat and positive. Finally, they had to learn enough about the lighthouse that they could step in for a tourist guide if the need arose. Sara had no idea how many others met all the eccentric terms, but she did, and she was accepted.

The cottage could have been expensive and should have been more than she could afford. But a nest egg had been saved for her by an aunt who wasn't Amish. Sara had been certain she would never use it. When she did, the guilt almost paralyzed her the moment she made the bank transfer at the realtor's office. But the nest egg was little enough, truly. She would do good with it. And she was no longer Amish.

"Look at you." Sara got up from the chair, went over and stared at her face in the mirror in the cottage's bathroom. "Such blue eyes and dark eyebrows. Blonde hair and black eyebrows—how is that possible? Not that you were ever vain about it. But still."

She read her German Bible for half an hour that first afternoon. Prayed. Then went outside the red wooden door that had a weather-stained brass knocker of an anchor she admired a moment. The museum had not removed it despite fear of theft or vandalism. Something to do with a legend about good luck and God's blessing. She touched it, unsure. She walked around the stone cottage with its flower gardens and bright red window baskets. There was a sign on the cottage that named it Round Turn and Two Half Hitches. After that, she followed the worn flagstone path to the lighthouse which was two hundred yards away—locked. Only the crew who came and went and maintained the automated light had the key.

That didn't matter. There was a metal ladder, well-riveted from what she could see, that ran up one side of the lighthouse to the lantern deck. Signs warned people off and threatened prosecution. But since the end of the ladder was at least twenty feet off the ground, it would take an athlete to jump and grasp the bottom rung. Or there would need to be something or someone for a person to stand on. That night, she made a running jump and caught the end of the ladder on her second try. She hadn't expected to miss her first try. Jumping games like this had been common in the barns of the Amish when she was young. And she was still young. Only twenty-eight. She scaled the lighthouse and stood on the lantern deck while the powerful electric light blazed over her shoulder and out across the dark ocean.

"There be coastline here," she murmured. "There be rocks. There be dragons."

She stayed a long time watching the blackness. Now and then the lights of a vessel moved past from north to south or south to north. It was a warm April night without much of a breeze. Still, as midnight came and went, she hugged her jeans jacket closer to her body. Time for bed.

She missed the lowing of cattle and swirling fireflies and the clip-clop of Morgans pulling buggies home for the night. Though at one in the morning, everything would be as quiet there as it was on St. Silvan's. Except she could hear the waves. Ocean swells thumping into the rocks. Just before a sleep of deep greens and blues, like the song she shouldn't have heard as a teen put it. The sound of water lapping against a sandy beach made its way through the dark and the noise of the surf pounding the rocks offshore.

Who are you now, Sara King? What is your name? Tell us. Tell the seven seas.

Chapter Two—Sara, Not Sara

I wasn't able to stop myself from rising early any more than I could stop the sun from doing it.

I made myself coffee from the beans and hand-grinder I had brought with me. My navy backpack had more tools than clothing. I'd left all my dresses and shoes behind, including the ones on the train. Jeans and shirts and hiking boots were good enough. After a quick shower that was colder than I liked, I went outside to water the flowers and window baskets with the hose. I saw there had been a vegetable patch once, maybe for strawberries too, and thought about purchasing seed packets in the village. A white pickup was parked by the lighthouse, so I decided to go down and take a look. There was no one around but the door to the light was open. I waited, biting into an apple I'd brought along from a fruit basket. Someone had been kind enough to stock a few items in the fridge and cupboards too. I suspected the realtor. Surprisingly, she had bought items I could make use of—corn meal, oatmeal, whole milk and butter from a local dairy, apples, pears, carrots with their tops still on, and some decent flour. I had to remember to thank her. I was halfway through my apple, a green one, before a young man and a young woman in bright blue overalls came down the inside staircase and emerged into the morning. Both of them seemed a little taken aback. I responded to that with one of my best smiles.

"Hello," I said. "I'm Lyyndenna Patrick."

The woman, about twenty, looking to me like a college student hired on for the summer just as English neighbors did in Pennsylvania, finally smiled a bit. "Hey. We're just making sure the light is a hundred percent."

"All's well?"

"It is. Are you a tourist? I don't think they start doing island tours till after July 4th."

"No. I live here. At least, I live here now. I'm in the cottage."

She was a redhead with the freckles and jade eyes. The jade eyes widened considerably and took in all kinds of morning sunlight. "You bought it? You're Sara King? I thought she was an old widow." Then she went crimson. "I'm sorry. What a thoughtless thing to say."

I wasn't bothered by her comment. What stung was my boy Daniel's death. That was what hurt the most. Not so much the loss of Jacob, my husband, to be honest.

"No, it's all right," I told her. "I guess I look old to you."

She shook her head. "That's the thing. You absolutely don't. You look amazing. It's like you're a Harvard fourth year or something. You're totally young and pretty."

Now I was crimson. I knew I was. It felt like I could fry an egg on my forehead. "Thank you. You're too kind, really."

"It's the truth. I'm Kara Wingate."

"And you can call me Lyyndenna."

"I thought the woman buying the cottage was someone called Sara King."

"Yes. That's me. The old me, I guess. The old me from a million years ago and a million miles away. Please call me Lyyn. Or Denna. Or the whole name at once. But never Sara."

"So, you're not Sara."

"I am. I was. But now I'm Lyyndenna Patrick. Which isn't much of a stretch really. Patrick is a family name. Back to Revolutionary days."

"I like Lyyndenna."

"And I like Kara."

The young man with her, sporting a full-blown black beard, carefully trimmed, nodded his head at me. "Lyyndenna Patrick. Good name. I'm Tyler. Tyler Franklin. Welcome to St. Silvan's. You really need to come down to Breakers some evening. That's where everyone gets together. Even if you don't drink. That way you'll get to know the islanders before all the tourists show up."

"Hi, Tyler. So, how many tourists are going to show up?"

"Thousands. We have some pretty nice beaches here and some great hotels and restaurants. Even in the winter we get people from Boston and Cambridge and Salem. Of course, they'd need to stay a week because the ferry is only a Friday ferry then."

"And you both live here?"

They nodded.

"Except sometimes, I go to be with my parents on Scrimshaw," Kara added. "It's a small island just south of us in Massachusetts Bay. Maybe eighty people on it. Dad just comes and gets me in our boat."

"Spoiled," teased Tyler.

She stuck out her tongue. "Jealous."

"You get too many storms on Scrimshaw. And too many sharks."

"We get some of the nicest weather, and you know it."

I jumped in. "I read that about eight hundred live on St. Silvan's?"

Kara gave Tyler a fierce green-eyed look before turning to me. "That's about right. I'd say closer to a thousand now. Some take their own boats back and forth. In the winter, they'll work from offices in their homes if they can. What do you do, Lyyndenna?"

"Well. Right now, it's going to be writing."

"Really? Like with Harlequin or something like that?"

"Something like that."

"Wow. Good luck. What a perfect place to write, hey?"

Lyyndenna smiled. "I agree."

"There's another writer," Tyler spoke up. "Hawthorne. His place is a couple of miles from the cottage here. Old like yours but a bit fancier. It used to be owned by a sea captain in the 1800s. It's kind of an old, dark, rambling house."

Kara grinned, her eyes coming even more alive. "It's fascinating. And he's not the only one, right? Isn't there a group?"

"An artists' group. Yeah. Like I said, you really need to show up at Breakers, Lyyndenna. You passed it coming up from the wharf. It's made of all that cool driftwood and the planking from a tall ship. Old man o' war. It busted up at the lighthouse two hundred years ago. I forget who retrieved it for the tavern."

"Todd Smiths. Remember?"

"Oh, yeah. Todd."

I felt drained after they left. I hadn't expected to talk so much, so soon. Why had I been going nonstop? Why did I have to act like I was some NYC writer when all I was going to do was produce a weekly blog? Why did I even bring up my name change? Now it would be all over the island. The old widow Sara King is really the young widow Lyyndenna Patrick. God help me.

"Be quiet, Lyyndenna," I murmured. "You need to talk much, much less. This needs to be a quiet place. Prayer, mediation, your German Bible, gathering wildflowers and driftwood. Why talk at all?"

I made my way from the lighthouse along a path through tall sand dunes that were half grass and came to one of the beaches. White—like beaches I'd seen the one time we'd visited the Amish community in Sarasota, Florida. Once I got closer, I realized the white came from seashells the ocean swept against the southeastern shore. From my map of St. Silvan's, I remembered there was a beach called White Shell. This must be it. The beach spread for several hundred yards before it changed into a light-colored sand for a few hundred more. I bent down and put my hand to the shells. Some were crushed but most were only broken in half or badly chipped. They felt smooth against my palm. I tugged off my boots and socks and went barefoot. It felt fine, it felt good. I walked awhile, enjoying the sensation. Somewhere sometime, I'd heard a line from a poem--nor can feet feel, being shod. I'd been barefoot a lot as a girl. Time to go back there.

The day was not hot, the day was not cold. When I reached the sand, I paid more attention to several families flying kites with their children. The kites were all colors and all shapes. They swooped and spun and darted into the sun. I couldn't see the lines that held them to earth, so they appeared to be more independent than they were. I craved that independence. From my past. From the deaths of my husband and son. From the years of my husband's cutting words. From the manner in which my faith had been lived out under the Amish ordnungs.

Does God really care if I pin up my hair? Or wear a prayer Kapp? That my clothing has no buttons? That my dresses are long and dark? Does it matter to God whether the men have mustaches or not? That they have beards that must not be trimmed? Is it a matter of life or death that Martin Luther's Bible be used, that we only sing hymns in German, that Pennsylvania Dutch be the language we speak among ourselves? Does God say no cars or trucks? Does God say no airplanes? Does God say no electricity? Or do men say all of that? I don't mind leaving those rules behind. It is the friendships I miss. The faces that wrinkle with smiles. The honest laughter. The many kindnesses. Working together with the other women at a quilt, or at baking five hundred loaves of bread, or at preparing all the food for a wedding. I miss someone taking my hand and praying for me. Like the kites, I am free to roam. But only so far. They are tethered to their lines and to the hands that hold them. Just as I am tethered to the lines of my past and my faith and to the many hands that hold those. Lines that can be as taut as steel cable and hold just as firmly.

A kite broke free and sailed out over the ocean.

"Yet even the strongest line might not hold forever," I whispered.

A boy ran along the sand calling out to the green kite.

A bishop from another county had visited our church once.

His message had been unusual.

"Sometimes some of us leave the Amish path. It may only be for a while. It may be forever. It may be a mistake. It may be the Father's will. Despite what others may say or not say, you must answer to God for your decision, you alone. Listen to the advice of your church. Then pray and make up your own mind before the Lord. Only take this with you if you must go--simplicity. Ours is a simple life and a simple faith. Do not lose the simple ways. Or if you lost them before you left, go out there and find them again and bring them back to us."

I was not surprised the sea and its shoreline brought so much into my head. I had always longed for what the English called blue water, but rarely had I been able to go to it. The farm kept me landlocked. Had I stood by the ocean more than five times? How often had my Daniel seen it? Once, twice? So that it should stir the blood and free up my thoughts--I had expected that. I had wanted that. It's why I'd fled to St. Silvan's to begin with and not into the deserts of New Mexico or Arizona. Saltwater that stretched out far beyond what my eyes could penetrate. A sky that poured into the sea so there was no way of knowing where one began or the other stopped. I'd wanted infinity. That's why I went to the sea to discover what was unknown.

I was just thinking about using a gas stove for the first time that evening when the brass knocker sounded. It actually had a deep bell-like ring to it, making me think it might be hollow. I opened the red door, pushing my loose hair back from my face. It was Kara. Bubbling.

"Hey, I want to take you to Breakers, my treat," she said, everything about her a bright smile. "They have the best halibut and chips. I'll introduce you to everyone you need to meet."

I knew protest would be in vain, but I tried anyway. "Kara. That's so sweet of you. But honestly, I don't have anything to wear. And my hair's a mess. So, I'll say no--"

She cut me off with a laugh. "Oh, Denna, believe me, you are perfect just as you are. You couldn't be more perfect. You mustn't change a thing. It's Saturday night at Breakers on St. Silvan's, and you absolutely look the part."

Chapter Three—Breakers

I was in the sort of fix Grandpa King used to call a perpedoodle, making up his own Pennsylvania Dutch word. On the one hand, I just wanted to be left alone with the sea and sky and God. On the other, I did want to make some friends, and I didn't want to wait until the island was overrun by tourists. So, I climbed into Kara's green-like-her-eyes Jeep Rubicon and went hurtling down the road to the village, Kara talking like she drove, fast and nonstop. I wasn't at all ready for the interior of Breakers.

A dory hung from the ceiling, anchors and nets and harpoons from the walls, empty barrels and kegs were our seats and tables, brass lanterns our lighting. I wasn't quite ready for the crew seated around the barrels Kara steered me toward, either. Her friends and Tyler and his buddies, about ten altogether and none of them older than twenty-two. It wasn't just that I was a widow with a name change that was widely known. That I was Amish was apparently island news too, and all of them wanted to know about the farming, life without electricity, the Morgans, the buggies, and the commitment to nonviolence. I was surprised I did not mind sharing the Amish ways with them as I was still very upside-down about what I'd done. However, talking about why I'd left was another matter.

"So, I have just lost my son and my husband," I told them, sipping my Pepsi and picking at my halibut and chips. "Both were ... farming accidents. Both a year ago.

In March and April. I needed to get away. That's all. No, no, don't think the Amish community was insensitive or unsupportive. I just couldn't be there anymore. I needed a completely different place. I'd always dreamed of the sea, of being by the sea. So here I am."

"But why St. Silvan's?" asked Tyler, one arm around his tall, dark-haired girlfriend.

"Because of the cottage. I saw the advertisement in our paper in Pennsylvania for the lightkeeper's house, so I wrote the people in Boston."

"There were a lot of questions they put to you, weren't there?"

"Yes, there were."

"And you have a naval person in your family?"

"Yes. Coast Guard. An uncle. All the way back to the 1930s."

"What about the writer?" This from Kara.

"Serenity Grace Greenwood. Popular in her day but overshadowed by Louisa May Alcott. Who she met."

"Like *Little Women* Alcott?"

"The same."

"Wow. So, you write like them? Like Alcott and Greenwood?"

Right then and there, as I sprinkled more malt vinegar on my chips, I decided to give up the ship. "Oh, I need to explain about all that. I did write stories as a girl, and they were smiled upon. But when I wrote stories as a teen, writing was frowned upon. So, I gave it up."

"But--" from one of Kara's friends.

"I'll be writing a weekly blog. I'm supposed to be getting a new iPad for that from Boston. I pray that may lead to something more. Something like Alcott or Greenwood. I have no idea. It may have been bred right out of me by the *ordnungs*."

"What are those?" the friend asked me.

"Rules. Laws. Policies. How the Amish organize and govern themselves."

"Which doesn't include painting *The Last Supper* or writing books or playing the violin." said Kara.

"No. It doesn't."

"Is that another reason you left? So that you could try and be a writer like your relative?"

I shrugged. "Who can say what God has planned? If my son or husband were still alive, I wouldn't be here."

"Or what the universe has planned," Said Tyler.

"As you wish," I replied, popping a chip in my mouth.

"Hey." Kara sat up in her chair. "There's Hawthorne. And Sydney Ryder. And Scott Munro. They're in that artists' group I was telling you about, Denna. I invited them here to meet you. Come on. They're sitting down at another table."

"You mean another barrel."

"Hurry. Grab your plate and your Pepsi. I'll introduce you."

"I'm good where I am, Kara. I don't want to intrude on them."

"How can you be intruding on them when the reason they're at Breakers tonight is to see you?"

"I'm a blogger. An amateur blogger. Not even that."

"Wait until I tell them about Serenity Grace Greenwood and Louisa May Alcott."

"Kara, Kara, please don't."

I took the three writers in, and they were a quick blur of faces. Honestly, later on I couldn't recall the details, exactly how they looked, exactly how they dressed. I remember one of them saying I looked like an islander. Kara told me on the drive home that was because I was tanned, my hair was streaked, my denim shirt and blue jeans were faded, and I had the jeans rolled just above the ankles.

"I bought the shirt and jeans at a secondhand store," I told her. "All my English clothes are second hand. My tan? Well, it is a farmer's tan, what else? And the sun streaks my hair, not a hair salon."

"Well, Denna," Kara said as she drove, "I suppose it will embarrass you for me to say this. But it all comes together extremely well. You're truly a beautiful woman."

I lowered my head and felt the burning on my cheeks. "I'd rather you didn't say things like that, Kara."

"It's true."

"I ... I am not used to compliments of that sort. They make me uncomfortable."

"Surely men have--"

"No. It is not the Amish way."

"When you were dating--"

"We do not date. There is only the courting. All right, yes, yes, Jacob said sweet things to me in those days. But such words quickly dried up."

"Why?"

"You will have to ask him."

"I can't ask him."

"And I can't speak for him."

Sydney wanted to know about Serenity Greenwood. Apparently, her works were experiencing something of a resurgence. She had a new paperback of my ancestor's novel, *Three Shorelines,* and wanted me to sign it. They used SG Greenwood for her name. I knew the book, I knew all of Serenity's books, even though I wasn't supposed to. For the longest time, I wouldn't sign. But Sydney, a firecracker of a brunette, wore me down. I finally took the pen from her hand. To me, it was just a simple signature. To her, it was something fashioned in gold. She showed it around the table, and Hawthorne and Munro praised the curves of the letters and the broad loops of the capitals.

If I had been honest with them and Kara, which I was not, I'd have told them when I was a teen, and thought the bishop might let me become a writer, I'd practiced my autograph over and over again. I'd been caught and scolded for this and told to develop a signature that was plain. I'd thought my author signature was plain. So, I'd created something that made mama and papa happy. Which also meant not using my pen name of Lyyndenna Patrick, Patrick being my mother's maiden name as she was a convert to the Amish faith.

That night, I went down to the beach in the April dark. The crests of the waves gleamed. I began pitching pebbles into the surf. I was wondering if I'd fled the Amish because I couldn't stay where my son and husband had died or because I'd been restricted from being a writer and a thinker. Hawthorne had said Greenwood was superior to Alcott but had never received the breaks or reviews she deserved. Munro had agreed and quoted a line from Greenwood's *August*: *The light never got through. Not through the windows. Not through the doorways. Not through her gray eyes and into her mind. The years had smudged her and put a thick streak of charcoal over everything that had life. She did not know how to kindle another fire.*

"Brilliant!" he'd exclaimed. "You can't imagine how I'm looking forward to your writing, Ms. Patrick."

"It's blogging, sir, only blogging," I'd protested.

"I'm sure you've written something."

"I haven't."

A lie. I had. Munro seemed to be able to pluck that information right out of my brain. I had started the book at thirteen, hidden it at fourteen, thought about destroying it at fifteen, then resumed writing it at sixteen. Every now and then I had snuck it out and worked on it, right through my twenties, my marriage and motherhood. I'd brought it with me.

Munro the Magi. Yet all I could recall of him that night was his New England accent and that he wore glasses. And that he looked like pictures I'd seen of Stephen King. Hawthorne? I couldn't recall Hawthorne at all. But the lighting had been dim, the ship's lantern flickering.

Except. His hands resting on the table. Large. Rugged. Brown with sun and weather. Fingertips stained. From pushing tobacco into the bowl of a pipe, I suspected. Exactly like Grandfather Patrick's hands. Just younger.

I found larger pebbles and threw them too. Then stones. I was fighting something, but I did not know what. It was my young son, Daniel. How he would have loved to have been here throwing stones into the sea in the dark beside his mother. How he would have loved it. And my heart broke all over again.

Chapter Four—Mount Suribachi

May and June passed like the ocean passed by St. Silvan's—in a hurry. I fell into a routine of reading and blogging and watering flowers, wandering beaches and praying. On July 4th, the ferry began bringing hundreds of people to St Silvan's. It ran four times a day, and a second ferry began sailing a week later. There were seventeen beaches on the island, and half of them had hotels right on the shoreline, far enough back to keep them free of high tide and storm surge. The Independence Day fireworks were set off at the rocks a good distance from the lighthouse. The crowds were kept well back as yellow and orange and blue burst over the sea—all new to me because I'd never attended any July 4th celebrations. And though I'd seen the fireworks from far away, I'd never seen them explode in front of my face.

The tours began then too. Guides took people inside the lighthouse between ten and four, and they walked around the cottage too, though the guide kept them about a hundred feet away. I didn't know what to do with that. I wasn't the person to stand outside and grin and wave to hundreds of tourists. So, I hid indoors or made my escape between mobs to the library in the village or down to the White Shell. There were hundreds of tourists on the beach too, but at least I was anonymous there as I rolled my jeans up and waded in the sea.

I desperately wanted to swim, but I had no suit, and the ones I saw for sale in the village, I found immodest.

Kara to the rescue. It seemed she and her girlfriends were always at my side. They wanted to teach me to drive. They wanted to find me summer dresses I could live with—long ones with lots and lots of color. They chose the ball caps and sandals and the simple island jewelry of wood and bamboo I could actually say yes to. I was Amish Not Amish and trying to find my way in my new life and my new world.

The suit they picked out was a one-piece Speedo, modest enough except it was far too snug. The girls complained and remonstrated with me, but I was unmoved. I purchased one in black two sizes too large. It drooped a bit, and that was what I wanted.

"Oh, Denna," Kara moaned. "It's summer and you have a perfect figure."

"I want to go in the water," I snipped back, "not parade myself down a runway."

"Well, you definitely could parade yourself down a runway, Mrs. Patrick," said her friend Jazz.

"Lyyndenna, please. Or Denna. So, becoming a supermodel is not what God and I had in mind."

Kara put her hands on her hips. "I thought you weren't Amish anymore."

"I'm not. But there is still some Amish I want to keep in Lyyndenna Patrick."

"How much?"

"Enough yeast to make the dough rise properly."

"What?"

"Let's just go swimming. All of us. I'll pretend to be your mother, ha-ha. Take me to your favorite beach."

"Our mother?" snorted Jazz. "They'll believe one of us is your mother before they'll believe you're ours."

I had quite a time with the girls that summer. In truth, I did need swimming lessons as well as driving lessons. They took care of both. I suppose I could tell a thousand stories about learning to drive Kara's Jeep Rubicon. What a trusting soul she was. I almost went off the wharf twice and off cliffs into the sea more than I want to say. Though the time that made Kara and Jazz laugh the hardest (the cliff times were screams) was when I panicked and hauled back on the steering wheel like a pair of reins to make the jeep stop. It didn't work, and we bounced off the curb. The times we didn't go over the cliffs, Jazz said made her believe in an Amish God. The time I pulled back on the reins, she said made her believe in a God who enjoyed a good laugh.

The beach? Well, what can I say about swimming and the beach? I didn't mind drowning and tried it several times. It's not as if I hadn't swum in ponds and creeks and lakes. But ocean swells were something else. I had to use stronger strokes, kick harder, and hold my breath longer as I learned the crawl and the butterfly from Issime. She was a champion swimmer at Boston University and waitressing at Breakers for July and August. She had me using weights at the village gym, The Shoals, to put muscle on my arms and back and shoulders. So, by Labor Day, I was swimming better than I had my entire life. I surprised myself.

I surprised myself by buying a new Speedo too. The droopy one drooped too much. The undertow kept pulling it off. Not that anyone ever saw my Speedo struggles underwater. I was quite the aquatic gymnast, ha-ha. The girls were there to clap when I tried on a suit that fit like it should. But I now had the problem of swimming in a Speedo that fit like it should.

I was reminded of my girlfriend, Lydia Zook, who was always getting in trouble at sixteen for what the bishop called her "rock and roll dresses." It's just that she wore dresses that were slender and hugged her figure a bit. Which her mother never seemed to notice. Now I had a swimsuit the undertow couldn't touch but which made me look like Lydia in a rock and roll Speedo. My solution to the problem was to run out of the water at full tilt and dive into the biggest beach towel I'd been able to buy. Wrapped up in that, I looked like a pile of laundry. The girls harassed me about being a prude, but I didn't care. I had no desire to be St. Silvan's new center of attention. I just wanted to swim, lie on the sand, look for seashells, and live a simple, unobstructed, unnoticed life. Amish Not Amish.

So, by the end of July, I had a license and had been blessed by a local on the island who wanted to sell me his Willys Jeep from 1945. He had kept it in beautiful condition since he'd acquired it in Arizona in 2010 and had fought a winning battle against our saltwater climate. He also offered to be my mechanic as long as I owned the Willys, which I accepted. Mike was sixty-two and a Vietnam vet. He and his wife, Amy, became my dear friends. As did the jeep, which he'd nicknamed Bachi because it had actually been on Iwo Jima during the battle in 1945. (Mount Suribachi was where the Marines had raised the flag in the iconic photograph everyone knew about including my "no war" Amish church.)

Not that I knew anything about that except for the famous photograph. Mike had to explain Iwo Jima to me. There were three bullet holes just by the spare tire at the back of the Willys. "Nambu machine gun," he'd told me. I'd nodded. Of course. A Nambu machine gun. "They have to stay." I nodded again. Where would I take them?

"And it has to keep its sand camo. Ok?" It did have a paint job that reminded me of the color of light brown sand. I nodded a third time. "And it has to remain stock." Mike had a lot of faith in me if he thought I could customize a motor vehicle and give it chrome wheels and bumpers.

"Definitely, it will." I'd begun to pick up on the girl talk.

It was a standard. Kara's Rubicon had been a standard too. Just an easier kind of standard. It took a while. I popped and stalled and backfired my way around the island before I finally got the hang of it, but I was determined not to disappoint Mike. Why had he sold me his vintage jeep which had only ten thousand miles on it? He liked my online blog, which also got printed in the island weekly, *Spindrift*. I honestly don't know why anyone liked my blog. But he did. Especially the one about an Amish woman who'd only driven Morgan horses learning to drive a Jeep Rubicon off a cliff. So now Bachi and I were partners.

Mike wasn't the only one who liked the blog. I began getting all kinds of good feedback. So much so that papers in Boston picked it up. It was God. What else could it be? My editor at *Spindrift* was ecstatic and offered me a salary.

A salary! The whole blog idea had just been a requirement for being allowed to purchase the cottage. There hadn't been any income attached to the deal whatsoever. I'd been living off what was left of the nest egg, which I hoped I could stretch over two years before it was exhausted. Now Fwanya, from Namibia, was talking about five hundred dollars a week, but he wanted two blogs, one on Monday as well as Friday.

"Of course, I said yes," I told Mike and Amy at Inked, a coffeehouse in the village. "But. It's happening so fast. I'm farther away than I wanted to be this soon."

"Farther away from what?" Amy asked.

"From where I came from. From the Amish. From my past."

"How long has it been?"

"Over three months."

"You've told us you still believe in God, isn't that so?"

"Yes, yes, nothing about that has changed. I'm just trying to find a different way to live and express my beliefs."

"Then perhaps things are moving along as they should, Lyyndenna. It's still about faith for you, isn't it?"

"Of course. Yes."

"Then keep going that way."

"I will. I have to. I just don't always know what to hold onto from my past and what to let go. And I don't understand why my blogs should matter to so many people."

Mike smiled at me. "It's not just that you wrote a blog about learning to drive that amused me. We both like the way you mix your Amish memories and beliefs with discovering the island and Massachusetts Bay. It's an intriguing blend."

"Thank you, but to me it's a confusing blend. It's so difficult to work through what I've walked away from and what I'm walking into. I'm sorry that struggle is so apparent in what I write."

"How could it not be when you're so open? It doesn't make you odd or unpleasant to read. Lyyndenna, we are all struggling in one way or another. The blog is popular because you are a good writer, and you are an honest-to-God human being."

I hoped I was being honest to God. I felt like Sara King less and less every day. Yet I didn't feel farther from God or farther from my own soul. Just farther from what I used to be. Even though much of that still lived in me.

I had pored over the book I'd been writing since I was a teen, sure I'd be asked to share something with the artists' group besides my blogs. Which everybody could read anyway. I'd found out they didn't meet from May to September, so I began picking away at my book in August. I made changes and added new parts to the story. I didn't use my iPad. Just pen and paper. It was all pen and paper. Three notebooks so far. I was surprised by how autobiographical the book was. I thought there must be something wrong about that. But my pen and my mind kept writing that way. In a biography of SG Greenwood, there was a quote from her that helped. "All good fiction is, in one fashion or another, a matter of autobiography, of telling your own story through fictitious personalities and fictitious events. That's what gives it its reality and its power."

So, I carried on, sometimes thinking I knew what I was doing with my life and my writing and sometimes not. I drove Bachi everywhere, I walked everywhere, I cycled everywhere on my blue mountain bike, I laughed with Kara and the girls (who began including older siblings and friends twenty-five to twenty-eight for my benefit). I wrote everywhere too, in my head and in the notebooks. I visited all seventeen beaches and swam at each one. I got into beachcombing. I prayed at the seaside, I prayed in the moonlight, and I prayed watching the phosphorescence burn bright in the ocean. By September, I can't say I felt complete. I can't say I felt incomplete. I mourned my husband, but I cannot say I missed him. However, I mourned my son and wept over him every day.

In Amish romances, a man would have come into my story to save me. A knight in shining armor. I didn't want a knight in shining armor. I didn't want to be saved by a man. My life wasn't Amish fiction. I wanted to be saved by a God. One true, loving, kind-hearted God.

So, when Mark Hawthorne tried to be that Amish fiction savior, I wrote him out of the story. Or tried to.

Chapter Five—The God Game

The artists' group was not just a writers' group.

There were painters and sculptors and actors and musicians and dancers and poets and essayists. There were all kinds of artists of different races and different faiths. It was bewildering. I'd go away from the weekly get-togethers with my head in a spin. Yet I couldn't deny the meetings stimulated and inspired me too. They made me want to write and write in a way that was honest to God, not sugar-coated and glossed over and fuzzy-wuzzy. Not a rose garden without thorns. I'd never been able to talk about my secret book with anyone before, let alone as freely as this.

There were three basic rules. No politics, no religion (including the atheists who liked to say they weren't religious and then go on to tell everyone what they believed), no cruel feedback. Unless politics and religion were part of a character's story. I listened for the first two months and said very little. Finally, one Saturday morning before the end of October (we always went from nine to twelve and then had lunch together at Breakers), I had been asked to be prepared to share from my WIP (work in progress). About two dozen of us were seated in a circle in a large study room at the library.

I thought I'd be far more nervous than I was. I suppose if I'd had to read from my notebooks in June or July or even September, I'd have been stuttering. However, I was in a different state of mind altogether. I felt like I was dreaming my reading to them. I read for half an hour.

I was calling the book *Harvest* that Saturday morning. I told them I might call it something else by Saturday night.

There was this one thought that ate into Becca. If God was a father, was he anything like her father? Gracious and patient and kind? Well, how could God be? God was spirit. In the Bible, he roared and thundered and slaughtered Israel's enemies and broke people's hearts. Jesus was a better idea. Her father and Jesus were more like one another. Jesus was the father figure she wanted in her head and her soul. He was the one that said to love all her enemies. The other said to kill them.

And there was the suffering. Her two children dead as stones. Where was the love of God when they gasped for life after a truck smashed into their buggy? Where was the God who intervened and saved? She could never voice these thoughts aloud. But she thought about them in the long fields and in the barn with the horses. She thought about them before she fell asleep. Becca wondered if she would ever stop going over them. She wished she would. She prayed she would. It felt as if all the person she was and could be had been locked in chains and could neither grow nor be free until she resolved the issue of God and where God's love was or wasn't. The rain, at least, still fell, and the sun, at least, still rose, and the land, thank God, still turned every shade of green.

"How old were you when you wrote this?" It was a man named Erikk, who made sculptures with metal. "Didn't you say you've been working on this since you were thirteen?"

"I have," I told him and the circle. "I was about twenty-one here. I'd been married for three years and a mother for two."

"There's some lovely prose when you talk about rainfall and sunshine," said Munro. "It's poetic, and it works well with the heavier thoughts."

"Thank you."

"Let's hear something from later on in the manuscript. Let's see how Becca and your style grow together. Does this theistic issue continue to dominate?"

"I suppose we'll see."

It did. It does. Jazz was, not surprisingly when you combined her beauty with her energy and athletic ability, a dancer and part of the group. She made sure she sat with me at lunch. She wanted to talk about the part I'd read where Becca thinks she might be falling in love and is afraid. We actually took it to the beach, went for a swim, and then I dived under my gigantic towel before I froze. The Atlantic was an ice bucket in late October. Nevertheless, I would go on to swim at least once a week every month of the year. That's how crazy the sea air made me.

Jazz took off at one point to meet up with some friends at Inked but I stayed on at Northwest. I lay on my back and stared up at an impossibly blue sky that beat like a heart. I liked Northwest because it faced towards Gloucester and the shoreline so it was sheltered from the wind. I'd dressed under the towel and felt warm as a waffle. Not toast. A waffle. My son Daniel's expression. No, remembering did not make me cry this time. I smiled at the sky and one high white cloud.

I breathed in a scent of vanilla and tobacco. There might have been a hint of cherry. I recognized pipe tobacco because of Grandfather Patrick's smoking habits. I sat up and looked around but the smoker wasn't obvious. They should have been because the beach was half empty. What breeze there was came out of the south, so I walked that way, off to the left if you were facing Gloucester and the mainland. I still didn't see anyone.

"Your writing actually reminds me more of Virginia Woolf. With a dash of Melville. You're a thinker. A philosopher. It's not just about a narrative with you."

The smoker was behind a large boulder covered in seaweed.

"Mr. Hawthorne," I said.

"What surprises me is there is no bitterness. Angst but no bitterness."

I came around the boulder. Dark hair and dark eyes. Skin still dark from his summer tan. Khaki shirt and pants. A pipe I knew was called a freehand, looking as if it had been carved from a tree trunk. He had just successfully blown a smoke ring.

"I'm not bitter," I replied.

"But like Becca you felt you had to move on."

"There were too many associations with the deaths of my son and husband."

"And?"

"I needed to write freely. I realize that now. Without censure or condemnation. It's how I am working everything through."

"About God and suffering?"

"The love of God, God's absence, death, faith, loss of faith, all of that and more."

"I'm thirty-eight now. Exactly ten years older than you. In my twenties, I was a minister. Even while I was giving messages and trying to help others, I had questions no one could help me with. Finally, I had to move on from that. At least until I had figured things out."

"What things?"

"Well, some of the same questions you have."

"And?"

"I wrote my first novel. *Break Break Break*. From Tennyson's sea poem. Do you know Tennyson?"

"No."

"Yet you've read lots of other books an Amish woman wouldn't normally have access to."

"I felt compelled to use the library in our town."

"Openly?"

"Quietly."

"Have you read my novel?"

"No, I'm sorry, I haven't."

"It was on the *New York Times* bestseller list for three months."

"Lots of books are on that list, sir. Many of them are poorly written. You get on that list for selling a lot. Not necessarily because you're good."

"You're blunt."

"One of my virtues."

"Good is a matter of opinion, Mrs. Patrick."

"I'm not Mrs. Patrick. Lyyndenna, please."

"And I'm not a sir. Not with only ten years between us."

I smiled. "Fair enough."

"So, you haven't read my book?"

"Mr. Hawthorne, I didn't know you existed till a few months ago."

"Hmm." He blew out a cloud of creamy white smoke. "Perhaps one day."

"Perhaps."

I sat down on the sand facing him.

"One thing that happened for me, Lyyndenna, was reading the Bible and realizing it said I could also learn about God from the things God had made. It's in Romans."

"I know. The first chapter."

"Then I read in Matthew where Jesus changed the Bible. You know. 'You have heard it said but I say?'"

"*Ja.* Of course." Grrrr. I annoyed myself whenever I slipped into German or Pennsylvania Dutch. "'You have heard it said, love your neighbor and hate your enemy but I say to you, love your enemy.'"

Hawthorne went on. "So, for me, that changed a great deal in my brain. And in my heart. That is a very sweeping statement. It changes the Bible. All those nasty verses about killing Israel's enemies with vengeance no longer apply. They are not right. They are not true. That is not who God is. Jesus altered the whole picture. He set things straight. God is not slaughter and bloodshed. God is love your enemy. God is pray for those who persecute you. God is don't resist the evil person. God is turn the other cheek. Do you agree?"

Right from the beginning, Mark Hawthorne was so convincing. And interesting. And, unfortunately, attractive. Him and his rugged, handsome face and his flashing eyes. Ugh. Flashing eyes. I'd already put him in a romance.

"I don't know," I responded. "That's a lot to change with just a few words."

"To me, it's simple. Jesus says that verse is wrong, and he changes it. The verse has universal application. You can't have God telling you to wipe out your enemies, even the infants, say that's God, then say love your enemies is God too. God is one or the other. I decided to go with the change Jesus instituted. God is love, not hate. Simple. Are you opposed to simple? Perhaps Lyyndenna Patrick prefers layered, complex, and complicated?"

He made me laugh, and I didn't want to laugh. I didn't want to react to him in any positive way at all. I was totally frustrated with myself. "Simple is good if simple is true."

"You have left the Amish behind. Have you left Jesus behind?"

"No. And I haven't left the Amish behind either. Just parts."

"So, Jesus still matters to you?"

"*Ja. Na sicher.*"

"What he says makes all the difference to you?"

"*Ja.* Yes. Of course."

"That is what he said. What will you do about it? Hmm?"

I didn't respond.

He got to his feet and knocked his pipe against his palm to remove the ashes, then slipped it into his pants pocket. "Would you like to walk the beach a bit, Lyyndenna?"

No, as a matter of fact, I would not. I am perfectly fine here on this island without you intruding. But, I liked his voice, and I liked listening to what he had to say. So off we went. Grrrr.

"Would you like to play a game?" he asked.

A game? "No, thank you."

"From that verse in the Bible. In Romans. We can know what God is like by looking at the things God has made."

"How does that become a game?"

"What does the sea make you think of? Quickly. Don't overthink it."

"Why ... power."

"God's power?"

"Nature's power, God's power, yes."

"What about the sky?"

"The sky? Heaven. Peace. When it's a blue sky."

"Wind?" he asked.

I thought as fast as I could. "Wind? A strong wind?"

"Yes. A strong wind."

"God is spirit."

"Fire."

"God is intense."

"A breeze."

"God is gentle."

"Sand."

"God is infinite. His ways are infinite and past counting."

He kept coming at me. "Sun."

I had no intention of losing the game. "God is warm.

"What else?" he prodded.

"God is light."

"What else?"

"God is clarity."

"Stars."

"God is light in darkness."

"What else?"

"God is beauty."

"That piece of driftwood there."

"Just a minute." I seized his arm without thinking and then swiftly drew back, horrified at what I'd done. "Uh ... it's your turn. Not mine. Driftwood yourself."

"God takes what is lost and turns it into something marvelous. God restores."

"Salt air," I put to him.

"God is bracing," he responded. "God is invigorating."

"Seashells."

"Eternity. God is eternal, and we are eternal with God. Death cannot change that."

"Seagulls."

He laughed. "God soars."

I wish he hadn't laughed. A peculiar tingling silvered through my body. No, no, no.

"Uh. Thank you very much, Mr. Hawthorne. I must get going. And ... and ... we probably shouldn't meet like this again."

"Why not? It was a chance encounter."

"Nevertheless, Saturday mornings are sufficient."

"But, Lyyndenna, we're having an amazing time."

"Yes, yes, we are. Too amazing. I'm not used to social interactions with men. It's awkward. It's uncomfortable."

"You're not uncomfortable."

"I don't even know you."

"Well, how else do we fix that except by chatting?"

"I don't want to chat. I don't want to fix it. I'm a widow. I just want to leave."

"But, Lyyndenna."

"I have to leave. God knows I have to leave."

And I fled.

I ran all the way back to where I'd parked my jeep.

I was breathing so hard I waited five minutes to start the engine.

What a mess.

Chapter Six—Something Rich and Strange

I am not an unburdening person.

But I wound up unburdening myself to Kara.

I did not want anything to do with men romantically. Saturday morning and Breakers was enough. It was casual but professional. Whatever that meant. I did not want to be dated as the English dated. I for sure did not want to be courted the way we Amish courted.

"What do you want from men?" Kara asked me.

"Nothing!" I snapped. "I don't want anything from men. Except to leave me alone."

"Were things so bad with your late hubs?"

"What?"

"Your husband. Were things so bad?"

"No, no, they were fine. Oh, what a lie. He was very harsh with me. Very unkind. Thank God, I had Daniel at nineteen so I could pour my affection into him. And receive his in return."

"Don't you think the way your husband treated you has something to do with the way you're feeling about Mark now?"

"I don't feel anything for Mark."

"I mean the way you don't want to feel."

"I don't know. I definitely don't want another Jacob. And I definitely don't want another man. I don't want anyone."

"Well, I doubt he'll talk to you again except about writing. Not after you ran from him and left him standing there like a duh."

Hawthorne didn't talk to me. I'd had my hour and wouldn't have another till the new year. When I interacted with others in the group, he listened but never jumped in. He let others do that. He'd only speak up after I'd had my say about someone's art and water had passed under the bridge. At lunch, he sat with Sydney and Munro. And that's the way it went for three Saturdays. Hawthorne wasn't rude, and he didn't snub me. He just made sure he gave me my space. As Jazz put it.

That was what I wanted. I felt good. I blogged, prayed, walked the beaches, collected driftwood to place around the cottage, spoke to tourists now and then, drove Bachi to the cliffs to admire the view, sang hymns in German there where no one could see or hear me, weathered the storms as November ended with a howl, sat in on the Saturday meetings and enjoyed the talks given by landscape painters and photographers, worked on my novel. I knew eventually I'd have to get it typed into Word, but for now I was content to scribble away in my notebooks and leave the book like that. Sometimes the skies were navy and indigo, other times the color of steel anchors. I wrote on and prayed on regardless.

I have tried to understand what happened at the end of November. The very last day. I deliberately drove to Northwest, did what my friends called the Iceberg— jumping in the cold ocean—dressed under my towel and went exploring. I thought my wandering was aimless. Till I smelled the pipe tobacco.

You might think I'm making it up and knew exactly where I was going. I had no idea. The cliché applied to me—my head was in the clouds. The clouds were grey as mud and my head was stuck in them. The moment I took in the scent of tobacco, I started to go back. I thought that's what I wanted—to turn around and go back. Instead, I went towards the boulder and stepped in front of him.

"It's a bit like following the smell of cookie dough or baking bread," I told Hawthorne.

"This comes from a tobacconist in Boston. Pippin and Took is the shop. She calls the blend Sea Change."

"That's an odd name."

"It's from Shakespeare. 'Full fathom five thy father lies, of his bones are coral made, those are pearls that were his eyes, nothing of him that doth fade, but doth suffer a sea-change, into something rich and strange.'"

"So, the sea changes him into something rich and strange?"

"Or you. Or me. It can mean any big change, Lyyndenna. Like a caterpillar turning into a butterfly. Metamorphosis. Maybe the sea does it. Maybe a song. Maybe a book."

"Maybe God."

"Maybe God. But God usually uses something or someone."

I sat down on the sand and faced him like I had before. "I just want a friendship. Someone to talk with who understands what it means to write your life and feelings out in a book."

"Sydney or Munro could do that."

"No."

"Why Hawthorne?"

"I don't know."

"You don't need to worry about relationship or romance. I don't want a serious relationship ever again. And I don't believe in romance."

"Well, I feel the same way."

"Good. Then that's settled. The air is cleared. We can carry on with our sea change."

I smiled. I felt as light as air. "Into something rich and strange."

He fussed about a moment, relighting his freehand pipe. "Where are you with your epic?"

"My epic? Becca is working through her feelings about her Amish husband who was killed in a haying accident. It isn't feelings of love she's wrestling with. She feels guilty she is grateful he is not there to hurt her with his sharp tongue anymore."

"How sharp a tongue?"

"Carving knife sharp."

"Is she getting anywhere?"

"Not really. She is supposed to love her enemy. He acted like her enemy. She loved him when they were younger. Her love eroded over time as he became more and more strident with her. She doesn't know what she feels for him now that he's gone. When she was crying at his funeral, she was crying over what they'd lost, the years they'd lost, the kindness toward one another they'd lost. She doesn't know how to pray. The Bible is like a dead stick when she tries to read it."

"We should walk, Lyyndenna." Hawthorne kept smoking as we roamed the beach under a sky as gray as the sides of a warship. "What is it Becca wishes to achieve?"

"She? Or the author?"

"She."

"She would like to be reconciled to her husband. She would like to recover the love they lost for each other. Even in death, she wants this more than anything else."

"What about the children she lost?"

"She did not lose them. The love was always there. She is confident she will see them again, and the reunion will be beautiful. Although she cries over them, all her memories are wonderful. It isn't that way with her husband. There are good memories from their first few years together. But they are buried by the pain."

"Because they weren't able to have more children?"

"Yes."

"He blamed her?"

"Yes. Constantly."

"Can she forgive him?"

"She wants to. Very much."

"What does the island offer that your Amish do not?"

"I can write a book about my struggle. There is no shame in that."

He took his pipe out of his mouth and tapped it against his palm before slipping it into his pocket. "We have some potters in our group. Pottery can be made in two ways. Where each piece looks virtually the same depending on the theme--cups are identical, saucers, vases, pitchers. Or where pieces, even of the same theme, do not replicate one another--each cup is unique, each bowl, each vase. The first approach is manufacturing. The second is art-- especially when the potter is not exactly sure what she will get when she removes each piece from the kiln."

"All right. You're going to tell me it's the same way with books."

"Yes. Fiction can be manufactured just like pottery. Books can look the same when it comes to the covers. They can sound the same when you open them up and begin to read. The characters can resemble the characters in other books. Plots can be the plots you've experienced a thousand times. Many people like this sort of repetition in their fiction. They like it in their religion, and they like it in their life. It makes them feel comfortable and secure and that there will be no unpleasant surprises. It may not be true to life, but they don't want true to life. Just peace and quiet. The books are manufactured to give them the same experience over and over again. Just like getting the same sort of cup, the same sort of painting, the same sort of clothes. I pass no judgment. It is what people choose, and we all benefit from manufacturing. But when it comes to fiction, and you are trying to be honest to God in what you write, and you are not exactly sure what your book will be like once you work through the process and remove it from the kiln, that is art. The book will be unique. It will not be like another, though it may share certain qualities. It will be one of a kind in every way including the cover and the ending. Art not only surprises the audience. It surprises its creator. It surprises the writer and painter and photographer. You don't know how things will end for Becca, do you?"

"No. And I don't know how things will end for me."

It began to snow.

He looked up. "Snow is better than rain sometimes."

"When it's gentle, yes."

Chapter Seven— Amish Fiction

I wanted it to be real. I wanted it to be real for Becca, and I wanted it to be real for me. I remembered standing by an open door at one of the library rooms in Pennsylvania and listening to a chat with two Amish romance authors— one a woman, the other a man. What struck me was how real the Amish characters in their books had become to the people in the audience. They acted as if the fictional lovers were real. I thought they were crazy, the way they went on. Why did she do that? Why didn't he say he loved her? How come she's so reluctant to get close to him or go to a hymn sing in his company? I could not take it seriously. The English and their butter churn fictions about Amish life and how we fall in love.

Now, I found out differently. Becca was real to me. She not only took on a life of her own as I wrote her story, she took on a mind of her own. She did things I didn't plan. She said things that weren't in the script in my head. Sometimes, I knew exactly what she was going to say. Other times, I had no idea what was going to come out of her mouth. I wanted to understand suffering and how to comprehend it in the light of God's love and mercy. She had other ideas. Becca wanted to find true love again.

She felt she'd had it once, for one or two years, before her husband began to speak harshly to her and avoid her. After waiting what she considered was a reasonable amount of time after his death (six months), she decided to pray about a second husband. The man who seemed kindest was not Amish. However, she was determined he would become Amish.

It started when she was running for her buggy in a sudden thunderstorm in town. The buggy was three long blocks away, and she knew she was going to get soaked. Then she slipped and fell, causing her to cry out as her hip slammed into the pavement. The bishop and his son were suddenly there, helping Becca to her feet and guiding her along the sidewalk to the buggy. Still, the rain was pelting down. Then it stopped. Only because a man was holding a large umbrella over the three of them. He held it over them until they had climbed into their buggy. Of course, he himself was drenched. The bishop shook his hand warmly. Becca did not look up but she memorized every detail of his face and smile regardless. She wondered if he would have come to her rescue if she had been by herself. She decided, yes, he would have held the umbrella over her head all the way to the buggy.

So, that was the man she began to pray about-- handsome, polite, gallant. She asked God if she might see him again. Her request appeared to be granted. The next five times she went into town, she spotted him each time. Once, Becca was in the company of the bishop and his wife, and the bishop waved him over. He introduced his wife and Becca. This time she smiled and did not drop her eyes. Oh, he was beautiful. Such a pleasant spirit. Samuel. She thanked him for his rescue. As the four of them chatted, he mentioned he was a member of the Episcopalian church. Becca thought, Well, Lord, soon enough Samuel will convert, and then he will be a member of the Amish church. A moment later, the bishop invited him to attend their church picnic the following Saturday and he accepted.

ME: OH, BECCA, FOR HEAVEN'S SAKES!

BECCA: VAS? WHAT IS THE PROBLEM?

ME: LIFE IS NOT THAT NEAT AND TIDY.

BECCA: SOMETIMES IT IS.

ME: I SUPPOSE YOU WILL MAKE SURE YOU ARE AT THE BISHOP'S PICNIC TABLE, JA?

BECCA: SO? WHY NOT? WOULDN'T YOU?

ME: NO, I WOULD NOT BE THAT FORWARD.

BECCA: FORWARD? HOW IS THAT FORWARD? THE BISHOP WILL INVITE ME TO SIT WITH THEM, AND I WILL ACCEPT. YOU ARE FAR WORSE THAN ME.

ME: I AM? I? HOW?

BECCA: OH, MY GOODNESS, HERE IS A BOULDER. OH, MY GOODNESS, SOMEONE IS SITTING WITH HIS BACK AGAINST IT GAZING OUT TO SEA. OH, MY GOODNESS, IT'S MARK HAWTHORNE, THE KIND AND HANDSOME WRITER. WHO WOULD HAVE GUESSED?

ME: I HAD NO IDEA WHO IT WAS THE FIRST TIME.

BECCA: WHAT ABOUT THE SECOND, THIRD, AND FOURTH TIME? ETC., ETC.

ME: I CAN'T BELIEVE I'M ARGUING WITH A FICTITIOUS CHARACTER.

BECCA: I AM NOT A FICTITIOUS CHARACTER.

ME: YES, YOU ARE. I MADE YOU UP.

BECCA: YOU DID NOT. I WAS ALREADY THERE. YOU JUST MADE USE OF ME.

ME: I MADE USE OF YOU? TO DO WHAT?

BECCA: TO TRY AND FIGURE OUT YOUR LIFE. I'M YOU.

ME: YOU ARE NOT ME. YOU ARE JUST AN IDEA.

BECCA: I AM VERY MUCH YOU. I'M JUST WAY AHEAD OF YOU. I KNOW I WANT TO GET MARRIED AGAIN. I KNOW WHO I WANT TO GET MARRIED TO. I'VE GIVEN MY FUTURE TO GOD. I'VE GIVEN MY PAST TO GOD. I'VE GIVEN MY PAIN AND SUFFERING AND CONFUSION TO GOD.

ME: I'M THERE TOO.

BECCA: NO, YOU ARE NOT, SARA OR LYYNDENNA OR WHATEVER YOUR NAME IS TODAY. WE'RE NOT EVEN IN THE SAME COUNTY ON ALL THIS.

ME: HEY. I DECIDE WHAT YOU SAY AND DO. I'M THE WRITER.

BECCA: NO, YOU DON'T. I'M THE CHARACTER AND I TELL YOUR HEAD WHAT I'M SUPPOSED TO SAY AND DO. YOU'RE JUST AN INNOCENT BYSTANDER.

ME: I'M INVOLVED.

BECCA: YOUR BUGGY IS FAR, FAR BEHIND MINE AND I'M PRETTY SURE YOUR MORGAN HAS THROWN A SHOE.

It was insane. Who was writing my book *Harvest*? Me

or my fictitious Becca? In a roundabout way, I brought it up with Hawthorne. He had a good laugh over that.

"Every writer talks or mutters or complains or pleads with their characters," he said. "Readers do the same thing. It's inescapable. Imagination can give the breath of life to anything and make it three dimensional."

"What if you have an argument with your character and lose the argument?"

"From the moment you wrote your first page as a thirteen year old girl, any plans you had for how your story was supposed to work went out the window. The same is true every time you sit down to create. The process and your mind and your fiction takes over. You race to keep up. Sometimes your plot is extraneous to what's really going on in the story and between the people who are in it."

"So, who's writing who?"

"You're just one of many authors, Lyyndenna, and not always the dominant one."

Well, all right, fine. In a second conversation, Becca pointed out that while I was still tumbling with pain and suffering and a good God, she had embraced that dark side of life. Jesus had legitimized it with his own suffering. So, had all the people in the Bible. And there weren't two Gods, one in the Old and one in the New. There was only the one. Jesus was the face of God in the whole Bible from Genesis to Revelation. You have heard it said but I say. He was the Living Word. He was it. His words finalized everything.

ME: SO, YOU BELIEVE ALL HAWTHORNE'S GOBBLEDYGOOK?

BECCA: I WOULDN'T CALL IT GOBBLEDYGOOK. HE'S JUST TRYING TO FIGURE IT ALL OUT. MOST PEOPLE

ARE COMPLACENT AND SWALLOW WHATEVER THEY'RE FED. JA? SO, MY BISHOP MUELLER BELIEVES THE SAME THING AS YOUR HAWTHORNE.

ME: HE IS NOT MY HAWTHORNE.

BECCA: JESUS IS THE FACE OF GRACE, THE FACE OF LOVE, THE FACE OF THE FATHER, THE FACE OF GOD.

ME: AND HE IS NOT YOUR BISHOP MUELLER. I INVENTED HIM.

BECCA: (LAUGHING) YOU DON'T INVENT ANYONE. YOU ARE JUST A WRITER. NOT GOD ALMIGHTY. BISHOP MUELLER WAS GIVEN TO YOU AND ME. YOU JUST WROTE HIM DOWN.

ME: NEVER MIND. IS IT TRUE YOU HAVE FORGIVEN YOUR DEAD HUSBAND?

BECCA: I HAVE.

ME: SO EASY, HMM? SO SIMPLE?

BECCA: THE PROBLEM WAS NOT SIMPLE, BUT THE SOLUTION WAS. WHAT ABOUT YOU?

ME: I'LL GET THERE WHEN I GET THERE.

BECCA: I THOUGHT YOU LIKED SIMPLICITY?

ME: I DO LIKE SIMPLICITY. I LIKE SINCERITY JUST AS MUCH.

BECCA: OH, I'M SINCERE ALL RIGHT. I JUST DECIDED I'D NEVER GET AN APOLOGY FROM A DEAD MAN. BUT I MIGHT FINALLY GET SOME LOVE FROM A LIVE ONE.

ME: REALLY.

BECCA: YOUR BUGGY IS STUCK. YOUR WHEEL IS IN A RUT. MAYBE IT'S BROKEN. ALL I KNOW IS, YOU'RE NOT GOING ANYWHERE.

ME: OH, WHAT DO YOU KNOW? YOU'RE A WORK OF FICTION.

BECCA: IF I'M A WORK OF FICTION, THEN SO ARE YOU. I CAME OUT OF YOUR HEAD.

ME: I THOUGHT YOU WERE ALREADY THERE, AND I JUST MADE USE OF YOU.

BECCA: I WAS ALREADY THERE. BUT YOU'RE THE ONE THINKING UP MY STORY. OR TRYING TO. YOU'RE STILL GETTING A LOT OF IT WRONG, AND I HAVE TO CORRECT YOU IN YOUR SLEEP. OR EVEN WHEN YOUR EYES ARE WIDE OPEN.

ME: IMAGINE IT HOWEVER YOU LIKE. YOU ARE NOT MY STORY ANYMORE. OUR STORIES ARE COMPLETELY DIFFERENT.

BECCA: THEY AREN'T. I TOLD YOU. I'M JUST WELL AHEAD OF YOU, THAT'S ALL. I CAN FORGIVE. I CAN ACCEPT SUFFERING AND THE LOSS OF MY GIRLS. YOU CAN'T ACCEPT LOSS, AND YOU CAN'T FORGIVE. BECAUSE OF THAT, YOU CAN'T SEE THE LOVE OF GOD. IT'S HIDDEN.

ME: I WISH YOU WOULD PLEASE STOP TALKING. JUST STOP. I'M TRYING TO WRITE.

Becca had a wonderful picnic. Samuel was a charming guest, in the best sense of that word, making magic and drawing people out of their woes, making the whole table smile and relax. Becca had made up her mind she was going to chat with Samuel as long as possible. She sat across from him and kept him engaged for the better part of three hours. The next day, Bishop Mueller dropped by to tell her Samuel had been to see him.

"He is interested in our faith," the bishop explained. "I promised to meet with him once a week and answer all his questions."

Her blue eyes sparked. "Why, that's wonderful. Isn't it?"

"Ja ja, sure, sure. It's wonderful if he's sincere."

"Why wouldn't he be sincere?"

"Because he likes you very much. And why not? You are sunlight, thanks be to God. But I mustn't judge. I mustn't jump to conclusions. He could be sincere about you and our faith both. You pray. I'll pray. We'll find out."

"Amen."

"Amen."

Becca was so excited she wanted to dance. But the Amish do not dance. Yet David had danced. And she'd decided Jesus would have danced at the wedding feast at Cana. So, in her kitchen, all alone, she danced after the bishop had brought her his good news. She danced until she dropped into a chair, exhausted and laughing.

"Praise God!" she sang out loud.

"Do we write the stories or do the stories write us?" Lyyndenna asked Hawthorne during a snowstorm walk the third day in December.

He managed to keep his pipe lit and puffed a few times. "You know how they say. Everybody has a story. Or as Anna Deavere Smith puts it, 'each person has a literature inside them.'"

"What does that mean?"

"It means you don't just have a story or write a story or have a story writing you. You are it. You're the story. All that you are. That's the book. That's the work of art."

Chapter Eight—Cappuccinos

Kara and Tyler and a work crew wrapped bulbs around the lighthouse. They had to keep them white so as not to confuse shipping. The mayor and council spared no expense. The tall column blazed like the Star of Bethlehem once the sun was down. Kara said the mayor would like permission to light up the cottage as well. I told her to go ahead. Christmas lights were something I never had with the Amish. I was also asked to join a caroling group that dressed up as if it were 1890 on the island, and I said yes to that too. Caroling was something else I was never able to enjoy in Pennsylvania.

"So, what did you enjoy when you were Amish?" Hawthorne asked me over cappuccinos at Inked.

"Oh, well," I replied, "I guess I still am Amish in so many ways. I like the quiet way of doing things. I like the German. I know many find it a harsh language, but I don't. I like the plain and simple way of living a life. We go at a horse's walking pace so much of the time. I like the emphasis on prayer. I like the emphasis on kindness and forgiveness. There is so much centered around God's love. So much centered around Christ's compassion and giving his life so we could have a good life to live. And, you know, I adore the horses. Not just the Morgans that drive the buggies. I loved watching the Percheron plow the fields and bring in the hay or the harvest."

"Would you go back?"

"I've thought about it, of course. A part of me expects the bishop and elders to show up here one day and coax me to return to Pennsylvania. Would I be persuaded? Maybe yes, maybe no."

"So, then, explain to me what hold the island has on you."

"The island? I suppose, well, the ways are simple here too. It's easy to find quiet spots and solitude. Easy to pray and think. And I can drive a jeep here, beachcomb here, look out over the wide rolling sea. In Pennsylvania, it's waves of grass—here it's waves of blue water and whitecaps. I like the people. I like the food. I like my cottage and my privacy. Hmm, and it matters a lot to me that I am free to write."

He paused to sip from a ceramic mug with his name on it. "And your novel is going how?"

I had to roll my eyes. "Ha. Well, I thought it was about me finding my way. But my Becca is finding her own way without me. She has no plans to leave the Amish behind, she has forgiven her dead husband, she's met someone she likes, and the love of God dazzles her."

"Isn't her story your story?"

"Do I look like a work of Amish fiction?"

"Well, Lyyndenna, the best fiction is almost always autobiographical."

"Who said that?"

"I did. And many others."

"Is it true? But I've been self-absorbed. Forgive me. How is work on your own novel going? Do you have a title?"

"Titles come and go, though they can help you focus on the main theme of the book. Today, it's *Gale*. Last week, it was *Storm Surge*. Tomorrow, it will probably be *High Tide*. I could also go with *Paean*."

"That's a big switch. *Paean* to what?"

"The lonely sea and sky."

"So, is that what the book's about?"

"It's about a person reaching out for a rediscovered life living by the sea."

Page 56

"Hey. That's what I'm writing about."

"I thought Becca was on the farm in Pennsylvania."

"She is. Her author and creator is here by the ocean trying to make sense of everything."

Hawthorne smiled that good smile he had. "Then I guess we're on the same page."

"Well. I think others have been there before."

"In one sense. It's a familiar theme. But that doesn't mean each story will be the same. It can be manufactured. Or it can be unique."

I paused a moment. Then blundered ahead. "I hesitate to ask this but is there ... is there romance in your story?"

"Why do you hesitate to ask it?"

"Because you said you didn't like romance. And because ..."

"You don't want to go there with me."

"Something like that. I'm sorry."

"Nothing to be sorry about. We both agreed on friendship and not a seashell more. As a matter of fact, Lukas is content with waves and sand and bowls of clam chowder. His last book was a thriller about the Navy Seals, and he doesn't want to write thrillers anymore. Even though that genre has made him a pile of money."

"So, then ..."

"So, then, he wants to write stories about transitions and transformations. People going into tunnels and emerging into the light."

"Metamorphosis stories?" I asked.

He drained his cappuccino. "Sure. Chrysalis."

"And no romance? Ever?"

"So far nothing like that. Why? What does it matter?"

"It's just that for Becca, I see that romance is a big part of her healing. She wouldn't be so far ahead of me except for recovering God's love and recovering man's love."

"Does a man love her?"

"No. And she doesn't love him. But it's leaning that way."

"Does it bother you?"

"A little. My main character is far more content than I am."

"Just remember that romance doesn't have to be slick and cheesy. It can be honest and true. Just because publishers might use it to bait readers doesn't mean the real thing isn't out there."

"Out there like the sea wind?"

"Out there like the seagulls crying."

I tinkled my glass of water with a spoon. "I want to hear something from *Paean*."

That smile. "I don't have it with me, and there's nothing on my phone."

"I'm sure you have something memorized."

"Are you?"

"I am."

He plunged right in.

It got to the point that any wave that touched the island touched him. Any breeze, any stiff wind, any gale. Every gull that perched, every ship that docked, every shell cast upon the sand. Whenever a big roller shook the black rocks, making them run with water like a beard, he felt the blow in his body. Soon he could not distinguish between the island and his own skin and body.

I honestly had nothing to say to except a pathetic "good work." It was more than good work. Hawthorne deserved accolades. I wanted to write like that. But how?

I decided to snub Becca and her romance and focus more on Christmas and the wild winter sea like Hawthorne was obviously doing with his novel. The village was festooned with all sorts of wreaths shaped like anchors, waves, gulls, and ships of every shape. The older section, which had buildings and streets from the 1700s, was literally dancing in holly with its bright red berries every time the wind gusted. Which also set silver bells tinkling and ringing that were hidden among the spiky green leaves.

The tall ship *Paul Revere* docked at our wharf for a week, its rigging flying the colorful signal flags the Navy relied on in times past, at night the same rigging streaming with Christmas lights of every color, some of them flashing and winking. Men and women in naval attire from the War of 1812 (a war even I knew New Englanders hadn't approved of and wouldn't participate in) formed up on the main deck every night, regardless of snow or cold or cutting winds, and belted out a mix of sea shanties and carols. I couldn't get enough of "Haul Away Joe" followed by "Joy to the World" and didn't miss a night. I bundled up in an old pea coat I'd found at Davy Jones with all its vintage clothing and marvelous antiques. The coat was two sizes too big, and I loved it that way.

I did my own caroling too as I'd promised I would. The outfit they gave me, a replica of a winter coat, skirt, and bonnet from the 1860s, in forest green, wasn't too big or too small but, like the porridge I'd heard about as a child, just right. Of course, I was used to singing without musical accompaniment, so caroling outdoors with just our voices was pure joy for me. It not only took me back to Pennsylvania, it took me back into a great warmth of the heart. We did this three times a week for most of December, and it never got old. Good things never get old.

But, from time to time, I had to leave the carols and wreaths and tall ship and roast chestnut vendors behind because I needed to go to sea again. Outside of my iceberg dips, I hadn't sat and gazed at the blue waters for some time. Waters, to be honest, which were sometimes steel gray or a kind of chilly raw green. The sea wind nipped and bit and cold spray chilled my face, but I embraced it all.

I was never a tropical girl. Our one visit to Florida was long enough at two weeks. I liked the Pennsylvania snowfalls and the sleet of New England. I wanted to be able to wear boots and sweaters and heavy warm jackets. I was a North Country Woman. Like Kara and Jazz and Issime and their friends.

There was one small beach that wasn't even listed with the other seventeen. It was only fifty yards long and sandless. I discovered it, you could say, by accident. I heard a long sharp rattling sound, like hundreds of marbles rolling over one another, and found a stretch of smooth stones, stones that fit nicely in my palm. Every time a wave came, it pushed the stones up. Every time a wave fell back, it drew the stones with it and created the smooth rattling sound. It wasn't irritating or unpleasant. It relaxed me. It soothed. As I had so many times on the island, I imagined Daniel beside me, and I knew how much he would like the round rolling stones carried back and forth by the sea.

It was only natural I should feel the sting. A mother doesn't expect to lose her son. Outgrow him. Outlive him. *You should be towering over me at sixteen. Picking me up in your arms as if I were no heavier than a vase of roses. Making me laugh. Bringing home girlfriends I don't think are right for you. Giving me grandchildren that exhaust me with joy.* Now it's a cold darkness.

But not for you. Not for Becca's two girls. You're in light. You're with a God of love. I have to trust something, and I trust that. I'll live and die with that.

Jacob. We had love once. We lost that love. You never lost God's. Everything I see in nature, in the sea, in the Bible tells me what is lost, God recovers. You too. Never in my Amish life have I believed that unbaptized infants go to a hell. It is not the Amish way to baptize infants or teach such a horror. Never have I believed that to take your own life is stronger than the mercy of God, the love of God, the strength of Jesus. You live. I should like to have been reconciled with you here. This is the best I can do. From here by the stones, I forgive you.

God. It's bitter for me some days. I'm not sure of myself. I'm lonely. I'm wind and rain and ice. I could not do this if you were not someone who knew pain. If you were above it all, my story would be impossible. Becca could not have mercy on her husband or be reconciled to the loss of her daughters. She could not love a man again. And if she can't, I can't. You are a man of sorrows and acquainted with grief. Isn't that how the English Bible puts it? That's my hope. That you have suffered like we have suffered. And know us. And carry us. That's my only hope.

The waves were still there when I fell asleep in my cottage, Round Turn and Two Half Hitches. The stones rolled up and rolled down and provided a rhythm for my dreams. When I woke up, I felt different. I picked up my mobile which I was beginning to use more and more. I texted Hawthorne. It was five o'clock.

ME: Are you up?
HAWTHORNE: I've been writing since four. Good morning.
ME: Can we walk and talk?
HAWTHORNE: When? Where?
ME: Once the sun's up. At White Shell.
HAWTHORNE: Just like that?
ME: Yes.
HAWTHORNE: What's so important?
ME: I don't know.
HAWTHORNE: Can't it wait?
ME: No, it can't.

Chapter Nine—I'm Not Here

Poor Hawthorne.

The sea wind reminded me of a hammer and anvil. It struck and sparked. A hard-blown spray coated our jeans and jackets and faces. Yet it seemed like I just had to talk to him by the open ocean in a cold gray dawn. Nothing else would do.

"Well, this is bracing," Hawthorne laughed. "You've really become an island gal, haven't you?"

I hadn't expected him to be that warm and forgiving about being dragged away from his cozy house and his writing. "I wanted to tell you in person."

"Tell me what?"

"I've made peace with the loss of my son. With my dead husband. With a God who has the face of a dead Jew. A Jew who isn't dead but knows what it means to bleed."

"That sounds like a lot."

"I guess it is a lot. Except, it's not complete."

"What do you mean?"

"I'm still angry about my life. Hurt. Disappointed with God. I feel like this island still isn't far enough away from my past. I need to get on a boat and go farther."

"Really?"

"Yes. Really. Maybe I need an island off the coast of Africa. Or off the coast of Vietnam. Or maybe I need another planet."

"So, you've accepted but haven't accepted?"

"I'm not sure how that works but yes. I'm content in my discontent. Or I'm discontent with my content."

"Now is the winter of our discontent made glorious summer."

"Who are you quoting now? I wish I did feel like glorious summer inside. I did for a while. I thought I'd resolved all this at Rattling Stones Beach. Honestly, I felt different inside. But I wake up, and I still don't understand the reason for putting people through suffering, especially suffering they had no part in causing. I don't understand why some women have experienced nothing like what I have, while others are exactly where I am--they feel like a sword has pierced their hearts. I don't like God's selective interventions--some are spared, some aren't, some are healed, others aren't, some are lifted out of darkness and many, too many, are left there. I hate to say it, but I feel like throwing a brick through God's front window."

Hawthorne could light his pipe under the most adverse conditions. He took his time doing just that, his back to the sea wind and to me. Then he blew white smoke that was immediately caught and carried away.

"You are a woman who not only values faith but clings to it. Yet faith does not mean you see everything and comprehend everything. It's very much a trust thing. You won't get all your answers here, Lyyndenna. You can't get all your answers here. You have to carry everything that's unresolved, believing there's more to it and that somehow the agony is a fit. That there's a purpose. That God isn't indifferent or malicious or void of love or powerless to make things right. Faith is about the invisible and the not yet and the incomprehensible. You know the prayer of the man with a desperately ill son in the Bible? 'I believe, help my unbelief?' It sounds like that's where you are. Not a bad place to be. Considering the outcome he enjoyed."

I was in a mood despite all his strong words. "I've never enjoyed that kind of outcome."

"No one can say what the outcome will be. It's the faith route, Lyyndenna. It's unseen."

For a flash of a moment, I thought he was going to put his arm around me as a fierce gust rocked us both. To my surprise, he didn't. To my greater surprise, I realized I wished he had. Inwardly, I kind of cringed. Now what was happening in my head?

I begged off going for breakfast at Breakers and drove to the cottage. I was about to burn my since-I-was-thirteen manuscript in the wood stove in the front room. Then I decided to retain it as an historical artifact and locked the notebooks in a drawer of the 1912 desk I wrote at. The desk Sydney Ryder called The Titanic. Because that was the year the ocean liner sank.

I immediately began a new manuscript. Typing it on my iPad rather than scribbling with a pen. I wrote the title, *I'm Not Here*, and the first sentences—

I'm not writing a novel. The novel is writing me. I have no narrative in mind. But a narrative is happening just the same. I am writing about what someone else is writing about me. I'm keeping track of the storyline. That's all I am doing. Running to catch up. I have no real idea of the plot or it's denouement. I'm just going to tell you about what I feel, what I think, what I pray, what I see and what I don't see. Scrapping Harvest. Becca has it all together anyways and doesn't need my meddling.

To begin again. *I'm Not Here*. Under the pen name of Lyyndenna Patrick.

At dawn, she went to the sea and told a friend about her struggles with loss and suffering and God and realized, like a breaker crashing completely open on the rocks, she didn't want him as a friend anymore. She wanted something more. It was an overwhelming thought she was by no means ready to receive. She denied it. Said no to breakfast with him and raced home in her jeep, driving sloppily, skidding on icy patches despite the winter tires. Without removing her pea coat or brushing off the snow, she sat down at her iPad and stared at the screen. Nothing came. She never had writer's block, but nothing came. Finally, she typed out two sentences. "It's not just the man. No woman is an island either, John Donne."

Which was the first thing I said to Kara after driving far too quickly to her condo in the village. "No woman is an island. I can't be that anymore. Don't ask me how I know about John Donne."

Kara stared. "What's going on? You look like you came in with the tide."

"I'll explain. But don't you--?"

"I have today and tomorrow off." Kara peeled off my pea coat, hung it, took my hand and tugged me onto a glassed-in balcony where it was warm as summer. "Sit. Exhale. I'll be back with coffees and some cinnamon rolls."

She had a perfect view of the harbor. The tall ship *Paul Revere* was at one side of the wharf, and people were standing in a long line ready to board and view it. *Revere* wouldn't weigh anchor for another two days. The wind was still up but not as raw, the sun was over the cloud bank, the bright signal flags snapped against the blue. I felt my body uncoiling. But I was still determined to say everything I felt I needed to say.

Kara shared the place with Jazz and Issime. Jazz was assistant manager at Breakers, and Issime was back from Boston U for Christmas break. Both were asleep.

Murray Pura

These Compass Rose units were new and pricey. Kara's parents had bought her condo for her, and she shared it with her friends who chipped in for utilities. I liked Jazz and Issime, but I was glad they were still in their rooms and under the blankets.

Kara was in her Snoopy pajamas. She came with the coffee and rolls. Swept a tangle of red hair back from her forehead and plopped in a big, fat, comfy chair facing me.

"What's the drama?" she asked.

I wrapped my fingers tightly around the coffee mug she'd given me. I liked the heat. But I didn't say anything.

She swept her hair back again. "No woman is an island. So, is that what you feel like you've been?"

"Yes."

"You have a lot of friends now. Me and the gals. The artists' group. Don't you and Hawthorne have a good friendship?"

"No. Yes. But no. No."

"What?"

"He's been so good to talk to. He's such a good listener."

"Totally. He's the nicest guy."

"I have to let him go. But how do I avoid him when we're both living on a small island?"

Kara stopped sipping from her mug and put it down on a round coffee table. "I must have missed something. Why are we letting him go?"

"He's too nice."

"Too nice?"

I blew out a lungful of air I'd been holding in. Time to stop shaflooting around. A word my mother had made up. "I want him to hold me in his arms."

This information stopped Kara cold. I got the big eyes, green eyes stare. "You do?"

I nodded once and held my coffee close enough to my mouth to cover most of my face. "Very much. Too very much."

"Umm. I guess I'm having trouble seeing the problem here, Denna. A nice guy. A nice woman. God or fate or the universe brings them together to give them some happiness. And the issue is––?"

"I'm a widow."

"So? Widows find new relationships all the time."

"It's only been eighteen months."

"How long do you want it to be?"

"Two years. Three years."

"What? Who told you that? The Amish?"

"No. Amish widows may remarry sooner than that."

"The Bible?"

"No."

"So, who?"

"Me."

"So, Sara King is alive and well and punishing herself. Why?"

"I'm not punishing myself."

"Do Amish widows take three years to remarry?"

"Not if God brings a good man to them."

"So, hasn't God brought a good man to you?"

I closed my eyes. "What am I supposed to do? Approach him? Women don't do that."

"It's the 21st century, girl. A woman can do whatever she wants."

"It's too bold. It's awkward. It's uncomfortable. And I have no idea about dating. No Amish do."

Kara bit into a roll and chewed a moment. "Do you want him or not?"

"I ... I would like to see if we could draw closer, yes."

"So, talk to him about it."

"I can't. It's too ..."

"Weird?"

"All right. Ja. It's too weird."

"It's only weird in your head. He'll be perfectly fine talking about it."

"No, he won't. He said he didn't want anything to do with romance. Friendship was all he was interested in."

"Yes, well, I'm sure he said that because he knew that's where you were in your thinking, and he didn't want to scare you away. Any man would be a fool not to take you up on an offer to explore the possibility of a romantic relationship."

"It's not what he wants."

"Why don't you ask him if that's what he wants today? Now? This Christmas?"

"How do I do that? I can't do that. I have no idea how to say I want him to hold me in his arms."

"Mark, I really want you to hold me in your arms." Jazz had showed up. "It's easy. Only eleven words. You don't even need German or Pennsylvania Dutch."

I made a face. "Easy for beautiful you, Jazz."

"Ha. Which should make it even easier for far more beautiful you, Lyyndenna."

I shook my head. "It cannot happen. It simply cannot."

Kara raised those dark, dark eyebrows of hers at Jazz. "Better get Issime in on this. We're going to need all the help we can get."

Chapter Ten—We Are and We Are Not

She spent the morning with the girls. It was all about dating and relationships and being real and being herself. In their words. She went away bewildered. And completely uncertain about the role she was supposed to play. Among the Amish, it was easy to court and be courted. Everyone knew what they were supposed to do. Out beyond the Amish farms and communities? Everything was out the window. There was no one way of doing anything. Let alone courting. Or dating. Or relationships. Or romance.

Romance. Was that truly what she wanted? She realized she had to be the one to broach the subject with Hawthorne. She had, in Issime's words, dumped him at least twice, "... leaving the sad dude on the beach with his hands in his pockets, the wind in his face, and his heart in his boots. No way in the universe is the guy going to bring up a romantic relationship with you. I don't care how uncomfortable you are, Denna. If you really want something to happen with this guy you're going to have to do the heavy lifting."

She brooded about this. Decided she either had to spill all to Hawthorne or forget about him forever and find another island. Like Martha's Vineyard, ha-ha. It had three.

She bit her lip and texted him a week before Christmas.
SHE: Hawthorne?
HE: 'Lo!

SHE: Can we get together?

HE: I just saw you Saturday at the group.

SHE: Ok, yes, I know, I mean another kind of get-together.

HE: A beach get-together.

SHE: Yes. That.

HE: Which beach? What time?

SHE: Northwest? In half an hour?

HE: I'll be there.

She waited the whole half-hour and a bit longer. Almost didn't leave the cottage. Then hurled herself into Bachi and drove to the beach. Her fingertips felt as cold as snow and her heart as rigid as cast iron. She took her time walking to the boulder covered in seaweed. Hawthorne was actually sitting on it.

"Hey." My new way of talking I'd picked up from Kara and the crew.

Hawthorne turned around and smiled. He was wearing an old army jacket in OD, olive drab. The sight of women and men in jackets like his was not uncommon on the island.

"Hey," he responded.

"Are you warm enough in that?"

"I am. It's got sheepskin lining."

"Would you like to walk?"

We headed along the beach. It was cold and quiet and still. Not yet lunch. He started chatting about Christmas Eve, so I knew I had to jump in or that's all we'd end up talking about.

"Hawthorne," I interrupted.

I think my tone was a bit strident. He stopped walking and looked at me. "What is it? What's the matter?"

All my careful plans about when I would say what, in a perfectly choreographed progression, flew away with the December wind. I had to give him the opportunity to say what he truly felt, and I didn't want to lose my nerve. I looked up at him, and I know very well I was looking at him differently than I ever had. Not that I thought about it at the moment.

"Is it difficult for you to spend time with me?" I asked.

Which was not what I intended to say. My brain and my tongue were clumsy. And now it was out there and up to him to deal with. I only regretted it sounded confrontational. But better that than nothing.

Hawthorne was perplexed. "Why ... what makes you say that? Have I given you cause to say that? I'm truly sorry if I have, Denna. You're a delight to be with."

"Truly?"

"Of course. Yes. Truly. What makes you think otherwise?"

"Nothing makes me think otherwise, Hawthorne. I just want to know if ... if you think well enough of me to take our friendship further."

"Further?"

This is getting more difficult instead of easier. Do I have to spell everything out? "You once told me you didn't want romance. Ever. With anyone. Do you still feel that way?"

I could see he was staggered. "Romance?"

Oh, Hawthorne! I am terrible at this. But so are you. Are you going to keep on repeating back to me everything I say? "Yes, romance, Hawthorne. Like in your novels. Like in your characters' lives. Is romance completely out for you? Do you ever, would you ever, do you think it would be something special ... if ..." I prayed and took the plunge. I might as well get it out and over with. He could call me crazy and we'd go back to our lives and iPads and loneliness. "If we had a romance of our own? A real genuine honest to God romance that was more than skin deep?"

Okay. Done.

I was still looking up at him as the wind picked up, and pieces of snow caught in our hair and melted against our faces.

So, I don't know what I expected, but I should have expected more from a writer because that's what I got.

"You have the bluest eyes." His voice had dropped almost to a whisper. But I heard him. "I've never given myself permission to really look at them until now. But you have the bluest eyes."

I liked the warm feeling his words gave me. Thank the Lord God he felt something for Lyyndenna Patrick. How much? Who knew? For that matter, how much did I feel for him? But no one other than my mother had ever drawn attention to the vivid color of my eyes. They simply were not plain. For years, I had hated their brilliance and felt they made me mawkish and ugly. Now I was having a new sensation altogether. Hawthorne was gazing so deeply into my eyes I felt his look penetrated to the red marrow of my bones. There was an immediate rush of pure happiness that made me almost cry.

So long. It had been so long since I mattered to anyone. So long since a man I liked had liked me back. I sank my head upon his chest. I didn't even think about it. It was either that or sit down. I didn't consider it bold or presumptuous. It was simply the most natural thing to do. Jazz had said, "Go with simple and uncomplicated. Go with natural and uncontrived. But go." The great gift came seconds after I closed my eyes over his heart. His arms slowly and carefully wrapped themselves around me, as if I were fragile, as if I might say no. If he only knew.

His great kindness was in those arms. His friendship. It was the thing I wanted most. I placed a mittened hand on his coat and chest. I was in seventh heaven. I didn't say it out loud but I wanted to be held a little tighter. Just a little tighter. As if he were listening, bit by bit his arms put more strength around me like a band of copper.

I snuggled. I burrowed. My cheeks shone with the quiet crying from my eyes. I felt safe. So safe. So wanted. I felt his lips gently press against my forehead. The wind struck and struck, but I didn't care. I didn't want to go anywhere. I understood nothing except that right now was the place I most needed to be.

It felt strange, strange, but the best kind of strange, a strange that did not paralyze, a strange that beckoned and enticed and exhilarated. If you thought I was going to pull back and run again, you had no idea of how his spirit drew me in and held me. His arms were wonderful but had little to do with my staying in his embrace. It was all that I felt far past his skin and muscles and bones. Far past his heart. The essence of who and what he was held me. The Amish would call that his soul.

At some point, we walked again. It snowed, it stopped, it snowed, it stopped. "Be a little presumptuous," Kara had advised, "but be presumptuous gently and a little secretly." My plans now were even simpler than they had been when I first showed up on the beach. I went with the flow of the tide. The tide within. I took his hand. I leaned my head against his shoulder. It made walking more awkward. I didn't care. It felt spiritual. It felt right.

I prayed to God he would not kiss me. I did not want that. It would break something. Everything was so fragile right now. We needed time to grow into something more. He must have felt the same way because the only kisses he ever gave me were on top of my blue knit beanie. I could feel those from far away, and I liked them very much. I suppose the biggest realization was that I liked him very much too. More than I thought I had. A seven, the way Issime put it, was actually an eight and hovering at nine.

"No, it's not a nine," I told her that evening at their condo in the Compass Rose building. "But definitely a solid eight."

Issime smiled. "Definite?"

"Definite."

"What's next?"

"Another long walk and then dinner at Bowline on a Bight."

"Ooooo," they all went at once.

"Fancy." Kara.

"Posh." Issime.

"He does like you," laughed Jazz. "All along he's had this secret crush he didn't dare talk about. Now he can cut loose, ha-ha-ha."

"Ha-ha-ha yourself," I fired back. "I'm sure he's nowhere as interested in me as you think he is."

Which I didn't think was true and certainly hoped wasn't true, but I'd learned to have the last word with that crew whenever possible.

Hawthorne understood I was still Amish enough not to enjoy posh. The truth was that Bowline on a Bight wasn't posh at all. It was old (I think 1745), brick, splendid with antiques, and the food was excellent. A little more than chowder and sourdough but, to be honest, the meal wasn't the highlight of the evening. It was a calm night, and Hawthorne drove us away from the village in his pickup so we could watch the Christmas stars glittering over a flat black sea. Then he took me to a church away and gone I didn't even know about, a simple white wooden church with a simple white steeple. It was locked, but he had a key.

"How did you get that?" I asked him.

"Well, the long story is my novel *Walking on Water*."

"I'd like to know right now. So, what's the synopsis?"

"I can do better than a synopsis. I can give you the two sentence blurb. Mark Hawthorne used to pastor here many moons ago. When I returned to be Joe Writer on St. Silvan's, they gave me a key, so I could pray here whenever I wanted."

"Now I want to read the novel."

"It's at the public library in Gloucester. You can have it sent here to ours and snag it."

"You were a pastor here. I'm amazed." I tried to read the sign in the dark. "What church is this?"

"St. Mark's."

"How appropriate."

"I thought so."

He guided me inside and flicked a light switch. Electricity at the snap of a finger was still something I was getting used to. I rarely used it at the cottage. The church was small, lined with enough wooden pews for fifty or sixty, had a sturdy pulpit carved like a wave, and stained glass windows lit from beneath that were fragments of blue. I adored the blue. Which I knew he knew. I sat down by one of the windows. Closed my eyes. Let my mind drift. Deep greens and blues, just like that song again.

"You're not going to fall asleep on me, are you?" Hawthorne teased.

I smiled, leaving my eyes shut. "I'm mediating. Just waiting for the service to start."

"It started the moment you walked in the door."

"Then I'm waiting for the message."

"The message? I don't do that anymore."

Be bold when it suits, the girls had coaxed. Boldness was in my nature. I was able to admit that eight months after leaving the farm. But not when it came to men. About whom I knew nothing. Nevertheless. "You'll do it for me."

I couldn't believe I actually said that.

Truthfully, I thought my feigned self-confidence was going to fall flat on its face.

I could feel the heat in my cheeks.

Then he began to speak.

I can't describe the storm of emotions that set off in me.

He really was going to do it for me.

I wasn't used to that from anyone.

Let alone a man I'd come to admire.

Still, I did not open my eyes.

"This chapel was built for fishermen and whalers and their families in 1699," he said. "Of course, it's been repaired and refurbished over the years, but it's still substantially the same chapel set on the same foundation. There was a garrison here once too, but its barracks and brick buildings were destroyed during the course of the Revolution. It changed hands many times so far as denominations go—Methodist, Calvinist, Baptist, Episcopalian. Now it's considered interdenominational. Various members of the congregation, women or men, speak on Sunday evenings when they gather."

I didn't respond.

So, he picked up where he'd left off. "I suppose you want me to say something spiritual and not just recite a history of St. Mark's. So, then it's this--we're all rebuilt and restored and renewed over a lifetime. There's fire and theft and storm and destruction. But we're built on the foundation we had from the beginning. Our body and our soul. Foundations are improved upon and strengthened. But it's still us with different windows and roofs and doors. In one sense, we are always ourselves from day one. In another sense, we aren't because we are constantly in flux and constantly changing. We are old, and we are new. We're ourselves, and we're different selves. We're still us, and we're altered versions of us at the same time. We are, and we are not. God help us."

I was thinking of Daniel and Jacob. I was thinking of the Pennsylvania I left behind. I was thinking of how good life had been during my twenties, and I was thinking of how hard and painful it had been too.

God help us? Yes, sometimes God's presence and blessing were obvious. Other times God was nowhere to be seen, felt, or heard. What did it mean to live and love by faith? To never see the unseen but still trust it? To never hear the unheard but still hear it? Did it mean to walk through the valley of death over and over again but fear no evil regardless of a constant shadow or grief or threat? What if there was no healing, never any healing, what if Jesus did not come by? Was my foundation truly still there being restored and rebuilt? Or was I a wreck built on sand and sinking, sinking, sinking ...

My tears were streaming down my face. I could not help it. I kept swiping at my cheeks with my hands, but it did not help. I could not stop the pain and bewilderment and loss.

"Denna," came his soft troubled voice. "Lyyndenna."

"Don't talk," I told him as I sobbed and choked. "There's nothing to say. Just hold me, Mark. Just hold me. Please."

I wept into his arms and chest and could not be consoled.

Chapter Eleven—Beautiful

So, if my story were one of the Hallmark Christmas movies the girls got me to watch, my life would have been put in order and healed by God and romance on Christmas Eve. If it were one of the Amish fictions so many read and enjoy, the result would have been something along the same lines. I know because I've read the Amish love stories. Three of them.

Few Amish read such books. Few English who read such books become Amish. It is a pleasant entertainment to them and, I pray, a spiritual encouragement. I do not begrudge them their innocent pleasures. But real Amish life is both beautiful and difficult, light and shadow, sweet and sour. It is a different path and for some, the best path. But no path on earth is free of stones and stubble any more than any bed of roses is free of thorns or every green forest, lovely as it may seem, is absent of poison oak. Yes, I know a number of the Amish romances are honest about that. God bless them.

Still, according to a typical Hallmark or romance storyline, Amish or not, Hawthorne and I should have kissed under the English mistletoe about the same time as everything dawned on me, and I understood exactly what God was doing and had been doing all along. Any bitterness or resentment would have been washed away. Or if not then, I would have been granted an extraordinary spiritual resolve to get me through and keep me going. I suppose if you wanted to stick to that script then Hawthorne was my miracle.

But he wasn't really. He was simply a good man who did not have all the answers or the keys to all the doors. He was my rock, for sure, as much as any human could be, but he wasn't God or the universe or the road through the valley of the shadow of death. We had to walk that together. Everyone has their own wounds and they seek their own healings. Including Mark Hawthorne. So that's what happened Christmas Eve and Christmas Day. That's what happened New Year's Eve and New Year's Day. Beginnings. Not endings and resolutions.

Besides. The whole week was a blizzard. In the books, the skies would have been crystal clear Christmas Eve. Or, if we did get snowed in, we'd finally be stuck together and kiss. Instead, we met in the storm New Year's Eve and walked by a raging sea, tightly holding hands as the wind beat and battered us.

"Would you return to Pennsylvania?" Hawthorne asked me, holding his head close to mine, so I'd hear him despite the howl.

"I might." I was just being honest. I wasn't trying to hurt him.

"Would you take up the Amish ways again? Pin up your hair? Wear the long dresses?"

"I might."

"So ..."

"So, no, I can't tell you what will happen next year. And you can't tell me. But I'm also being honest if I tell you I might stay on this island with you for the rest of my life."

"You might?"

He looked so hopeful. Like a puppy. I laughed and patted his cheek. "You're too sweet for me. Ja, I might. Just as you might return to Pennsylvania and convert. So much is possible. But I confess. The crooked places in my head and heart need to be made straight and the rough places plain before I'm going anywhere. Whether that's a geographical location or a relationship."

"What about us then, Lyyndenna?"

"Us? This is us now. Life isn't a movie or a storybook, is it? Things don't come to completion in one reading or in two hours. We have a lot to talk about, don't we? It will take time. But please don't look so worried. I'm ready to take the time. And I want to be with you, Mark. Take a moment to look at what my eyes are saying. I want to be with you."

He stared past my frozen eyelashes and laughed. "They certainly are saying something nice to me."

"Good. I'm glad you're picking up on what Jazz would call my vibes, ha-ha. Are you picking up on anything else?"

A fierce blast tore my knit beanie from my head and sent it spinning off into the sleet and dark. I squealed as the storm grabbed a hold of my hair and played with it, streaming it behind me like the mane of a palomino mare. I could almost hear the wind laugh in a silly, happy, boyish way. I could certainly hear Mark Hawthorne's laugh. It was the same kind.

"Yes, I'm picking up on something else." He was smiling, trying to catch my hair for me while it ran and looped through his hands like a golden rope. "You're beautiful, Lyyndenna. The most beautiful woman I've ever seen. You're more beautiful than the ocean. You're more beautiful than a dream."

END PART ONE

Part Two (January–June)

Chapter 12—Pennsylvania Plates

The bishop came at the end of January.

I knew he would come. I dreamed it. The same way Pilate's wife knew Jesus shouldn't be touched. The same way Paul saw a man dressed in clothing unique to the Macedonian world saying, "Come to Macedonia and help us." The same way Joseph knew to rouse his wife and child and flee to Egypt. Dreams are their own language, and they talk to us. I've always believed that. A number of Amish do.

The day was crystal. A beautiful blue sky. Which Hawthorne had told me on our morning walk was still far less blue than my eyes. Ha. The charmer. I'd hugged his arm and leaned into him.

"Keep it up and I shall fall head over heels for you. Isn't that the way you English say it?"

"It's an old expression, but yes, people still say that."

"So, what is a new expression?"

"You'll need to ask your friends Kara and Jazz and Issime."

"Anything else you wish to woo me with?"

"Woo? That's pretty old as well."

I pouted.

"But old or new," he went on quickly, "I do have something I'd like to add."

My nose might have been tilted. "Such as?"

"The sun is not essential. Because every day your hair is the sun. Clouds cannot touch it. It always shines. Always. And always gives us light."

I rolled my eyes and laughed. "Oh, that is so much corn you just shucked, Mister Hawthorne. But it doesn't matter. I happen to like corn. And what you said to me is so romantic."

BECCA: SEE? AND YOU TALK ABOUT MY AMISH ROMANCE.

ME: MINE IS NOT CONTRIVED. IT REALLY HAPPENED THAT WAY. HAWTHORNE REALLY SAID THAT.

BECCA: WELL, MINE REALLY HAPPENED THE WAY I SAID IT HAPPENED TOO.

ME: IT DIDN'T. YOU THOUGHT IT UP.

BECCA: YOU THOUGHT YOURS UP TOO.

ME: I DID NOT. FROM THE BEGINNING OF *I'M NOT HERE*, I SAID THE BOOK WAS WRITING ME, I WASN'T WRITING THE BOOK.

BECCA: YOU'RE JEALOUS BECAUSE I'M SO MUCH FURTHER AHEAD THAN YOU. SAMUEL HAS BEEN BAPTIZED AMISH. WE'RE GOING TO BE MARRIED.

ME: WELL, LA-DE-DA.

BECCA: HAWTHORNE WILL NEVER BE BAPTIZED AMISH. NEVER.

ME: WHO SAYS HE NEEDS TO BE? WHO SAYS HE HAS TO BE AMISH FOR ME TO MARRY HIM?

BECCA: OH, HE WILL. YOU'LL SOON BE BACK IN PENNSYLVANIA HOEING WEEDS IN YOUR GARDEN. THE BISHOP WILL SET YOU STRAIGHT.

ME: I'M PUTTING YOU BACK IN THE DRAWER. AND LOCKING IT.

Murray Pura
I'm Not Here

The bishop rapped on Lyyndenna's red door with his knuckles. He did not use the brass knocker forged like a ship's anchor. She saw through the window his wife was with him and another elder with his wife. And Eve. Her best friend. Who she'd told everything. Written three times from St. Silvan's. Sharing all her news and thoughts. Begging Eve to tell no one where she was.

Lyyndenna welcomed them in. She looked to see if there was a buggy with Pennsylvania plates parked behind them. It was habit. Of course, they had not come all this way by horse and buggy. The five of them hung their winter coats on hooks by the door. All of them were dressed in black. Eve, a silver blonde, looked stunning in black, of course. She always had. Now, she offered Lyyndenna a small smile.

Lyyndenna struggled. She asked God to forgive her but she could not stop herself from shooting Eve a piercing glance. Lyyndenna knew how ferocious her blue eyes could look when she turned them into thunderheads. Eve looked away. The bishop caught the tail end of Lyyndenna's glare.

"Please, Sara," he admonished her in Pennsylvania Dutch. "Eve was only trying to help us."

"How? By betraying my confidence?"

"We needed to know where you were."

"Bishop Zook. If I'd wanted you to know where I was I could have told you myself."

"Let us be calm. May we have coffee? Then we should pray."

"All right." Lyyndenna nodded. "I just ground some beans an hour ago. Arabic."

"You use a hand grinder, I see."

"Even after nine months I am still not comfortable with electricity."

Actually, I did not glare at Eve. I wanted to but didn't. My story wrote me like that. It's what came into my head and flowed through my fingers onto the keyboard. However, I truly could not look at her. Not for the longest time. *Ja ja,* forgiveness, forgiveness, as if it's so easy. Sure, forgive. But it takes time. More than the time for coffee and a chat.

And why were her parents with her? The elder, Thomas Mueller and his wife, Anna, were Eve's mother and father.

"We are staying at The Bristol," the bishop said as we sat in my parlor.

They used up all my chairs. Made sure to keep the conversation in Pennsylvania Dutch.

"The Bristol? Because it's old fashioned?" I asked.

He smiled. "Well, it looks old fashioned. But the oil lamps actually use electric bulbs. I understand they are concerned about a fire. What is it? Wood from 1897? We are comfortable, thank the Lord."

I grew a bit worried. "How long are you planning on staying here?"

He shrugged and poured himself more coffee from the carafe. "It is the Father's will."

"What is the Father's will? Whether you stay two weeks or two years?"

He held up a hand. "It's probably good that we pray before we talk anymore."

He prayed in German. The six of us bowed our heads. When I lifted my eyes at the *amen*, Eve's met mine. She

Page 90

began to smile a smile of conciliation. I wasn't having it. Not yet. I shook my head.

"So," the bishop said. "You've left us."

I decided to get right into it. "Outside of several of the *ordnungs* that make no sense to me, I have no argument with my Amish church and friends. This is between myself and the God that actually exists. Not a God made by human hands. Not a God made by churches or denominations or board meetings or pastors or bishops. I must get as close as possible to the One who truly is God, and who is far removed from our conceptions and imaginations and our wishful thinking."

The bishop's wife, Mary, spoke up. "It is best you stay with the church and the teaching to ask such a question. Only then will you find the truth you seek, Sara."

"I've been with the church and its teaching all my life, Mrs. Zook. The answers to the questions I'm asking now are not there. Just accepting what is, well, that's not good enough for me. My heart needs to journey. My soul needs to explore."

Eve mustered the courage to address me. "You wrote that you realized you must trust. That you had to walk by faith, walk by what cannot be seen but only trusted."

"Yes." My tone was January. "I wrote that to you in confidence like everything else. But it's not as if—" I snapped my fingers. "—I understand God and the universe just like that. Why does God answer some prayers and ignore other prayers? Why does he ease the suffering of some but not the suffering of many more?"

The elder, Thomas Mueller, shook his head and his long white beard. "Always the Father answers."

"Of course. Yes, no, or not yet."

"Exactly."

"Yet Jesus didn't say that to people. It says he turned no one away. What of that?"

Mueller shrugged in his black suit. "That was then."

"And this is now? Well, Elder Mueller, with all due respect, then or now is not good enough. I must find the God who keeps the promises he makes. Not avoids responsibility."

"That is our God. The God who keeps his promises. The true God."

"No. I need the God of the psalmists. Not only the ones who cry praise but those who cry pain. I cannot do that with you. *Ja*, we sing the hymns of suffering from the Old Country. But I don't want to sing those hymns without expecting some healing, some day, in some way. I don't want to sing and sing and sing with no end to my questions or grief."

"Not all questions can be answered here. Not all grief can be assuaged."

"Some questions must be answered, and some grief must be assuaged. There are too many noes and not yets. Or not evers. This is a path I need to take without anyone saying to me, oh, you mustn't think that, oh, you mustn't say that. I have to be free to voice all my questions without being rebuked or silenced or fixed—everyone rushing to pray over me so that I don't think those thoughts or say those things anymore."

Okay, I was venting. At them but it wasn't about them. They had been good to me. But there were Amish and Christians from other churches I knew who did act the way I'd been describing. I'd heard their voices and their words. I chose to stop my rant, as Kara would call it, and immediately began apologizing. "I'm sorry, excuse me, I'm sorry, I—"

"Stop." The bishop cut in. "We are not made of crepe. You wish to be honest. Go ahead. We will not stop you or, as you say, fix you. Have you ever read Psalm 88?"

"No."

"You should do that. Take the Lord into the darkness with you. Then the fear and pain is not as great." He got to his feet and the others with him. "May we visit you again tomorrow at the same time?"

I was surprised they were leaving me alone so soon. "Yes, of course, Bishop Zook."

We all shook hands after they had tugged on their coats. I even shook Eve's hand, which was a bit of a breakthrough, especially since we hadn't talked things over, and I absolutely hadn't forgiven her. The five of them walked along the path to the road, black figures against the white. There was very little snow down though. Just enough to sparkle.

I'd had a premonition I'd have a visit from Bishop Zook so I couldn't act surprised about that. I wasn't. I was surprised by my vehemence. By my bottled-up anger. Which I thought I'd unbottled. Apparently, there was a lot left. Or I'd opened another bottle.

I was too restless to write my blog for my editor Fwanya, his paper *Spindrift* and the *Boston Globe*. I threw on my peacoat and blue knit beanie and headed outside, pretty much marching. I went past the lighthouse and into the dunes to White Shell. The tide was high. Some new shells lined the edge of the beach. I found one that was whole. It hadn't been chipped or broken. It hadn't even been scratched.

How could a shell be tumbled about in the ocean swells from perhaps hundreds of miles out and hundreds of fathoms deep and show up on a shoreline unscratched and unscathed? I put it in my pocket. This would be my good luck piece, my blessing from the sea. I stood closer to the saltwater and let the spray from a huge breaker shower me, the icy drops cutting into the skin of my face. I waited for another.

When I'd first arrived on St. Silvan's, I'd been swept up in the power and majesty of the sea like the closet romantic I was. Then living life had snuck in behind me. Not that living life had been so bad. There had been plenty of beach walks, after all. But at the beginning, I'd let myself be pulled right into the sky, right into the vast expanse of rushing waves and shrieking gulls. I had danced in the dark with God and the night and the phosphorescence of the rollers from England and Ireland and France.

The dancing was not very good. What did my Amish feet know about it? Once I'd even stumbled and fallen headlong into the surf. Ha ha. It had all seemed funny to me and I thought: *Ja, sure, funny to God and Kara's universe too.* Now, somehow, I had lost some of that sea spirit. I didn't want my visitors from Pennsylvania to take any more of it. What little I had left needed to be replenished not diminished.

There was no one else on White Shell on a nippy January day so I made the most of my privacy by making a fool of myself. If I'd thought to bring my beach towel, I'd have had my weekly iceberg dip. As it was the blown spray and sea foam made a fine mess of me. Which is what I wanted. To feel.

The visit from Pennsylvania had put darkness into me. Not because they were dark people, but because they came to me from a dark place. A place where I'd lost my child and my husband, from that one spot on earth where my beautiful eight-year-old boy had been killed. The sharp memories gave me a trapped feeling. I wanted to be free of the grieving. Live some kind of life again that wasn't bits and pieces of good. Would God continue to seem close to me on one day and then far away the next?

The truth was I'd been gaining some ground until the bishop and his brood had showed up. They reminded me how much I'd lost and how much I'd given up. They also reminded me they were content with their vision of God. In the months before their arrival, I'd been doing better and making myself at home on St. Silvan's. I'd had some success seeing a God I thought I could not see in the bleak hours—it was all about trust and not prayer answered the way I wished it to be answered. Now I even felt disjointed from that.

I waded into the sea up to my waist. It was freezing. I didn't care. Waves struck hard. I staggered but remained upright. Ice formed on my eyebrows and eyelashes. On my lips. I didn't run. I wanted to feel something other than grief and doubt and confusion. I wanted to feel something other than a faith I'd accepted simply because I'd grown up with it. The cold of the winter ocean penetrated to my marrow. I bit my lip. I needed the January sea.

It seemed to me my whole body was still tingling a day later. This time, I was not in a ferocious mood when I met with the bishop and his crew. My whole body and spirit were in a place of peace. I listened and smiled and when they pushed me on returning. I simply replied that God had brought me to St. Silvan's. God was speaking to me in a different way here and using all sorts of different things to get my attention. If I was going to clear anything up with my life and a God who was often enough invisible to me, that was going to happen here as well. They saw the tranquility in my eyes. Heard it in my voice. I knew they did. So, I was sure they'd leave me alone and in God's hands. They did. But God's hands included Thomas Mueller's hands and his wife's, Anna's, hands and those of their daughter, Eve.

"They will stay on until the end of the month," Bishop Zook explained. "That will give you and Eve a chance to catch up. You do not need the older ones standing over you all the time, hm? This is a better plan."

"Eve is going to stay?" I was dumbfounded. I just wanted her to leave me alone. We could sort out her betrayal in our fifties.

"Yes. She and her mother and father will remain at the Bristol. It is my belief you and Eve will sort out everything you need to sort out between yourselves. This will bless you both. And when two are blessed and reconciled the entire world about them is blessed and reconciled as well."

I stared at the bishop. "It is?"

He nodded and rose to his feet along with his wife Mary. "This you will see, Sara."

There was an anger in me.

They could not make me do this.

They could not make me forgive Eve on their clock instead of mine.

I could have told them all to go back on the train together. I was not under any *ordnungs* on the island. They could not tell me who I must or must not spend time with. Not anymore. Not ever.

I was simmering with good heat when they passed by me and out the door. Only Eve lingered a bit. I will give her this. Eve always had courage. I remember the time she alone stopped a runaway Percheron when the rest of us thought she'd be crushed to death. I think my eyes at that moment were black as a twister cloud and far scarier than a Percheron running wild. Nevertheless, she met my gaze with her rich gray eyes, eyes that now looked stark and haunted, and did not cringe. She even straightened to her five-eleven height, two inches taller than me. I found it impossible not to admire her strength in the face of my death mask.

"Try," she said to me. "One time. One walk along the shoreline. Just try. For the sake of what we once had."

I knew my eyes snapped with forked lightning. "All right."

Chapter 13–Eve and Me

I confess I wanted to rub it in.

Eve was just a bit younger than me. There were four years between us and we shared the same birthdate--a Leap Year. February 29th. We'd always celebrated together since she was ten and I was fourteen. But I had married young at eighteen, and she had never married at all, and she was twenty-four.

That didn't matter to me. My marriage hadn't been a shower of gold. What I wanted to rub in is that Eve had wanted to stay in *rumspringa* forever, her Amish do-anything-I-want time as a teen, for two reasons: clothes and cars. Now she came to preach to me? I had both, and she didn't, and I was going to make sure she knew it.

It was a mild winter day. I chose a black leather jacket, black leather gloves, high black boots and warm black stockings with a sweet embroidered pattern, a stylish black skirt that came down just above my knees, then added dash with a royal blue cable knit sweater, a royal blue scarf, and my tossed-on royal blue knit beanie. I even used blue eyeshadow and blue eyeliner, and I knew my blue eyes were like blue skies. I was going to kill her. The only thing I didn't touch? My lips.

"You sure this is what you want to do?" asked Kara at her Compass Rose condo.

I was adamant. "Yes, it is. She ratted me out and now I'm going to make her squirm."

"How is you looking like a super model off the runway in NYC going to repair your relationship?"

"She loves to dress like this. She aches to dress like this. Yet she comes here to tell me to give it all up and return to Pennsylvania to be plain like her? We'll see who wants to be where. Another week with me on the island, and she'll begging me to let her stay and be Amish Not Amish for the rest of her life. And wait till she sees my jeep. She loves to drive. When I pull up at her hotel it will eat her heart out."

"Umm. This doesn't quite sound like you."

"Why doesn't it quite sound like me?"

"For one, you're not mean. For two, you're not mean. For three, you're not mean."

This kind of hit me. "What ... what are you ..."

"And for four, you're not showy. You dress down, and you dress simple, and you look sensational just the way God and the universe intended. Now it's like you're competing with yourself. Fighting with your own good looks."

My mouth actually hung open. I didn't know how to respond.

"Let me do this," Kara went on. "Let me wipe off your eyeshadow and eyeliner. Give you a black Aran sweater and a black scarf. We'll leave the skirt and stockings on. The leather jacket can stay with me for now. I'll put you in my army coat with the fleece lining. What size are your feet?"

"Nine. Sometimes nine and a half."

"Good enough, 'cuz I'm a nine. I'll grab my Wolverines for you. The 1000 mile ones. Very cool. Totally comfortable."

"No. Those are too expensive."

"The grays were only ninety-nine bucks. Just put them on and let me check you out."

"I can't wear hiking boots with my skirt," I argued.

Kara made a face. "Of course, you can. Who says you can't?"

"I would look foolish in our town in Pennsylvania."

"You're not in your town in Pennsylvania. You're on an island in Massachusetts Bay. You look just right. You look funky."

"I look funky?"

"We need to do something with your hair. Have you ever had a crown braid?"

"No, I have not."

"Stand over here by the mirror, *por favor*."

I did as I was told, feeling out of my depth with Kara and her vision of who I should or should not be with Eve. She fussed with my hair, braiding it in a circle about my head, put her hands on her hips, eyed me carefully in my new gear which was her old gear, and made the pucker kiss at me. "You'll do."

"Well, hey, thank you very much." I talked more like her and her friends all the time.

"Yeah, well, whatever package I wrap you in makes no difference at all to your impact, Amish girl. You still look like the AC/DC song "TNT." You know—dynamite!

"What?"

"I'll play it for you sometime. You should get going or you'll be late. Especially since you're walking."

"Wait," I protested. "I want her to see my jeep."

"No jeep. Keep it simple. Avoid the bling."

"Bling? It's a World War Two Marine Corps Willys that's been shot up by a Nambu."

"What the heck is a Nambu? Go. The Windsor's only three blocks from here."

I felt like I'd been scolded by my mother. I trudged petulantly to the Bristol, barely lifting my booted feet. This was nothing like I'd planned. I should be driving the jeep and alighting from it in all my glory. No, not very Amish and, as Kara had driven home, not very me. But for whatever reasons, I didn't just want to impress Eve. I realized during my short walk I wanted her to crave the freedom I had.

She was standing in front of the old white pillars of the Bristol. In black from head to foot including a black winter bonnet. She looked so innocent and pure and fresh like a gentle snowfall on a patch of dark earth. My love for her suddenly broke through the concrete of my anger. Eve Mueller. My childhood friend. I'd opened my soul to her for fourteen years.

She saw me approaching, her hands in black mittens clasped at the front of her long black coat. Neither of us smiled.

"Do you want to sit somewhere?" she asked, face white from the cold and whatever fear came from the heart. She spoke English.

So, I spoke English too. "I want to walk," I responded and led the way down to the harbor walkway which, if you followed it to its end on the left or the right, put you on a pebbly shoreline.

Rules had changed for the winter ferry. It now came and went twice a day. It was docked and letting passengers board as we walked past. It would head to the mainland at eight for the benefit of those commuting to work from St. Silvan's. There would be another run at six, in the dark, bringing islanders back. Then it would dock overnight until the morning sail.

"Do you go to Gloucester or Boston often?" Eve opened the conversation. "Or New York City?"

"Not really," I replied. "Until January 1st, the ferry only ran once a week. Now apparently there's a demand for a couple of sails a day. Maybe I'll take more trips now."

"I like your outfit."

I was kind of surprised. "Truly? It's pretty ragtag, isn't it?"

"It's pretty. Ragtag has nothing to do with it."

"Well, then, thank you. And your look is classic."

"Huh. My look is Amish."

"It may be Amish, and it may be plain, but it's still strong and absolutely striking. It rocks."

"It rocks? All your sentences sound so different from the way you used to talk."

"I suppose I am different. Altogether different. It will be a year this April since I came to St. Silvan's. I'm an island girl now, Eve. Like the song."

"What song?"

"Oh, a modern song my friends played to me. I have a number of friends your age. We get along well even though I'm four or five years older than they are."

"That doesn't surprise me. You and I have always gotten along." Eve stopped abruptly and placed her hand on my arm. "You need to understand. The only reason I told the bishop where you were ... it was because I wanted to come here. I knew they'd take me with them."

I was unconvinced. "That was the only reason? Or were jealousy and envy part of the mix?"

"No. I wanted you to be happy. But I wanted to see the world that was making you happy. I'm not here to persuade you to return, Sara ... Lyyndenna. I'm here because I want you to persuade them to let me remain here with you."

"What?"

"Believe me, it's no surprise to my family or Bishop Zook. They know I'm going to talk to you about this."

"They know? And they approve?"

"I'm twenty-four, and I'm not married. Am I so unattractive and such a bad cook?"

"Unattractive is not a word that can be applied to you."

"I'm not married," Eve explained, "because I don't want to be married Amish. I don't want the barns and buggies and bonnets and butter churns anymore. I don't know if I ever wanted them. I've told them all this. Children are raised Baptist and Pentecostal and Lutheran and

Episcopalian all around me in Pennsylvania. That does not mean they remain in those churches. Some choose to become Roman Catholic. Others choose to convert to the Orthodox Church. Still others turn aside to atheism or agnosticism or even paganism. Ja? So, children raised in Amish homes don't always want to be in an Amish home and church for the rest of their lives either. Remember Lydia? Rachel and Rebecca and Ruth Yoder––the three sisters? Thomas Miller? They all left to create lives that were ... well, to use some of your new language, to create lives that were authentic. Ja, authentic to themselves. You did it too. I'm not in some tangle with God the Father over suffering like you are, Lyyndenna. I'm not in a tangle with God about anything. I just want to live out my faith in a different way and in a different place. I'm desperate. I wanted them to bring me here, Lyyndenna. And I want your approval and their approval to stay."

She grasped my hand. We had always walked hand in hand. Even after my marriage. Even after I became a mother. She squeezed my fingers tightly. I hesitated. Then I squeezed back.

"Ouch." She winced but grinned that beautiful winsome grin of hers. "You're still a strong Amish farm girl."

I found myself smiling back. "I am. It's just that now I'm standing on the beach and harvesting seashells."

"Well, the beach is just ahead. Let's keep walking."

Our boots crunched on the ice-rimed pebbles.

"I wanted so much to yell at you," I admitted, giving her mittened hand another sharp squeeze.

"I prepared myself for it. There haven't been many fireworks so far."

"I realized this morning that I love you too much to hurt you more than I have. I'm sorry."

"Sara ..."

I didn't want to linger there. "Are you honestly prepared to live here as a single woman and find work?"

"Ja. Yes. Yes, for sure I am."

"And you like everything you've seen about the island so far?"

"I like the island very much."

"You say your parents and the bishop expected you to approach me about all this?"

"They did. They do. You must understand they are not completely opposed to this arrangement, Lyyndenna. Disappointed but they will not stand in my way."

"Why on earth not?"

"Because they know how unhappy I am. Because they know I am not turning my back on God. And because you are here."

"Because I am here?"

She leaned her head on my shoulder as we walked. Another old habit. "They love and trust you. Just as I do."

"This is all so strange and startling. I can't imagine them acceding to your wishes."

"Do you accede to them?"

"Do I?" I thought about this a moment. Then gathered her into my arms and gave her a huge hug. "I can't believe everything I'm hearing but yes. If it means I can have my BFF back then yes, yes, and yes."

She hugged me in return. "*Gut. Sehr gut.*"

I still could not accept it. "Surely the bishop will stand in our way."

"He won't."

"I need to speak with him but now he's back in Pennsylvania."

"No, he's not. He never left the island."

"*Vas?*"

"He knew we would talk eventually. He also expected you to agree to help me get started here. And that you would want to speak with him after I told you everything."

"Huh. Our wise bishop."

"Ja. And our friendly bishop."

"Ja? No ordnung talk?"

"*Nein.* He and his wife and my parents just want me to walk with God. They want me to retain my faith in Christ. Whether I'm in Pennsylvania or Massachusetts or on the moon, they can live with it, so long as I do not throw away our Lord."

I remained somewhat mystified. "That is surprising."

"Is it? Were you truly fleeing them?"

"You know from our letters I wasn't. It was more along the lines of me running to than running from."

"Then why does their kindness surprise you?"

"I just thought ... they'd fight harder to keep you where you are. And try to drag me back to Pennsylvania with them."

"Well, you'll see, my sister. *Mein Schwester.* We should head back to the hotel. The four of them are waiting on us."

So, they had bacon and eggs in the Bristol's restaurant. Eve too. I confess my appetite wasn't sharp. I was bewildered and confused. I had a bran muffin with a pat of butter and a cup of Scottish breakfast tea. The table conversation continued to bewilder and befuddle. All in Pennsylvania Dutch, of course.

"Of course, we would prefer you both live among us in Pennsylvania," Bishop Zook told me, sipping a French roast as black as his winter coat. "But sometimes we are not called to the Amish Way. Or we are not called to it until we are in our forties or fifties. Who knows the plans of the Father? But if both of you remain close to the Lord, and close to the Scriptures, we must be content. This is, however, a walk of faith for us too, for myself and my Mary and for Eve's parents."

Elder Mueller buttered a burnt piece of toast. Which was how he liked his toast to be. "Eve is a woman. She has long since ceased being a girl. She does not need our permission to do anything or go anywhere she pleases. Thus, we are grateful she continues to respect us and our bishop and cares about what we think. By the same token, the Lord would have us care about what she wishes and thinks and to respect her. So, this is where we are. Are you able to help her, Sara? Are you able to help our Eve settle in, find a new life she is happy with, stay on the path of God the Father?"

He made it sound so momentous. But I suppose it was. "I am. If that's what she wants, Elder Mueller."

"Oh, it is what she wants, certainly. But is it what you want? You were angry with her."

"I'm not angry with her any longer. I understand why she did what she did."

"Then there is the matter of God. Your anger with God."

"My confusion. My disappointment. My hurt. I continue to pray. To seek. To ask. To knock. To go through the doors that are opened to me."

"So, you continue to find?"

"Ja, I continue to find."

I had not walked with Hawthorne for several days. We met at White Shell that night. I poured everything out. He stuffed his pipe with a blend called Blue Water. There was no wind, so he had no trouble lighting it. The scent was rich, like roasted hazelnuts, the smoke creamy and white, the stars sharp and bright. And I was upset.

"I feel like they are expecting me to fix everything," I complained, "and I'm not that good."

He puffed calmly, as always. "Fix what?"

"Fix what? Eve. Find her a husband, find her employment, find her the right God, find her a place to live, find her new clothes."

"She doesn't really have a problem with God, does she?"

"Well, no. I guess that's on me."

"And can't she live with you for a while?"

"Yes, two are allowed to live in the cottage. She can stay as long as she likes. We're back to our happy selves with one another."

"I don't think you're expected to be a matchmaker either," he advised.

I raised my dark eyebrows. "No?"

"Does Eve act like she's desperate for a man in her life?"

"She doesn't."

"So that's not an issue either."

"Perhaps not. But men are going to notice her."

He smiled. "Men notice you. How could they not? Yet you stand before me."

Him and his quotes. "What?"

"I mean, you remain intact."

"I'm strong willed."

"She isn't?"

"Hmm." The answer was obvious to me. "She can be stubborn and determined."

Hawthorne plunged on. "As for clothes, I'm pretty sure she will have that in hand. Take her to Davy Jones for vintage. Gloucester and Boston for something new. You said she enjoyed dressing up during her wild and free period of life."

"Her *rumspringa*? Ja, she adored clothes and cars."

"So, just lead her to water and she will drink."

I leaned my head against his shoulder, and his arm went around me. "I think you're telling me I'm overreacting."

"I think I'm telling you there's nothing to worry about. I'm sure she's a sturdy and mature Amish woman. She will find her own way just as you did."

"You haven't even met her."

"You love her. She's your best friend forever. Right? What else is there to know? If you like her that much she is sure to be a marvelous human being."

I laughed. "Okay, ha ha, I guess so."

"And we all know what a tremendous judge of character you are," Hawthorne added.

"Yeah?" I imagined myself standing like Kara with a dead look on my face and my hands on my hips. I didn't have that face though and my hands weren't where hers would be.

"Not to mention that in you we find everything worth looking for."

I rolled my eyes. "Oh, we do, do we?"

"We do. Just ask anybody."

He could always reach down to some place far and away inside me and find a smile I'd lost. "All right. I'm asking you."

"Words fail me," he replied, pipe in hand.

"Ha. Since when do words fail you?"

"Here and now. Under these January stars by this January sea."

And he gathered me in and held me. Gathered me in and held me the way I'd come to love being gathered in and held.

Chapter 14 – Martin Luther's Bible

Absolutely everything went off perfectly once Eve and I became *roomies*--Kara's word. So, who used the bathroom when, what food we stocked the fridge and cupboard with, what we cooked, teaching her to drive, shopping for clothes in Gloucester and Boston, walking my favorite beaches, meeting my girls, introducing her to Hawthorne, Jazz getting her on her feet as a waitress and then quickly as a hostess at Breakers--absolutely nothing was a problem. Not even experimenting with makeup and hairstyles. It was what Jazz called our *spirituality thing*--that was the snag.

I still sang the old German hymns for sentimental reasons and because they were about suffering. I still prayed in German. Still read from my German Bible. Eve wanted nothing to do with any of it. She was at the small kitchen table, spreading chunky peanut butter into the troughs of celery sticks, when she decided to clear the air. It was two weeks into our new living arrangements.

"The Reformers were nothing wonderful," she suddenly spouted. "They murdered our people. Tortured and imprisoned them. Tore children away from their parents. Burned men and women alive. Oh, you want to be baptized as adults? Ja, sure, we'll baptize you again. So, they'd throw us into the lake with weights chained to our bodies and drown us. By the hundreds."

Probably by the thousands. I knew the gruesome stories. "It's the 21st century now."

"Luther was just as cruel and cold hearted as any of them." She bit into her celery and peanut butter sticks. The stuff smeared her mouth. I marveled not for the first time how she could look so cute eating like that. "He persecuted us. He persecuted everyone who didn't believe like he did. Are you aware he wrote all kinds of nasty things against the Jews?"

I didn't. "How do you know?"

She chewed and swallowed and wiped her lips with a napkin. "Google it on Wikipedia. I picked up several books on Luther and the so-called Reformation at the library back in Pennsylvania. The Nazis used what he wrote as propaganda to get the German people behind their slaughter of the Jews. The man disgusts me."

"Easy. Easy. Love. Forgiveness."

"Oh, hush, Sara ... Lyyndenna. I have no idea why the Amish use Luther's translation of the Bible, but I want nothing to do with it anymore. What sort of example is he? Just remember I'm not a widow. I never lost a husband and a son like you. I'm not sitting here trying to figure out why God the Father didn't intervene to save my family while I eat celery and peanut butter. Though I would be if that had happened to me. What I'm trying to say is you weren't running away from the Amish when you left two years ago. I am. That's the difference between us. I don't want those old ponderous hymns anymore. I don't want to wear black as if I'm constantly preparing for my own funeral. I don't want to do without cars or trucks or TVs or electric lights. What's the point? What does it prove? Does it make me more spiritual? And I certainly don't want anything to do with Martin Luther. Especially his Bible and his theology and his attacks on the Jewish people. I want a different life and a different way of looking at God than I've had for the past twenty-four years."

I saw a chance to calm the kitchen down. "Almost twenty-five."

She stuck out her tongue. "You'll be as old as Lancaster dirt. You'll be twenty-nine on the very same day."

I sat down at the table with her and began to peel a green apple with a paring knife. Stars glistened in the window behind her head.

"So, does this mean you're the new Martin Luther in the house?" I asked.

Eve's pretty silver eyebrows came together. "What? Me?"

"Does it have to be your way, or you'll burn me at the stake?"

Her face blazed scarlet and vermilion. "No. No. Of course not. I just get carried away. My rant, ja? I want to be free, Denna. That's all. Free to worship God and live my life in a way that is true to my soul and my spirit. I don't wish to take away your liberty to walk where you want to walk. Just don't ... please don't ... draw me back into the Amish ways. Don't expect me to pray in German with you or sing German hymns with you or read that Martin Luther Bible with you. Yes? Are we all right with that? Umm ... and I will not expect you to do what I do."

I popped a white sliver of apple into my mouth. "Kara would say, *Sounds like a plan.*"

"And what would Hawthorne say?"

"Oh, he'd quote somebody famous. Like Shakespeare. *This above all, to thine own self be true, and it must follow, as the night the day, thou canst not then be false to any man.*"

Eve laughed her silver laugh. "Ha ha. How do you know Shakespeare?"

"Since I've known Hawthorne. What do you think? As soon as I realized I ... well, that I ... as soon as I realized ..."

"That you liked him? Why is that so hard to say, sister?"

"I don't know." My ridiculous cheeks were burning and me at almost twenty-nine years old. I pressed a cool apple slice against them. "Anyways, yes, I bought a book of famous quotations of Shakespeare's and I dip into it all the time. I'm ... uh ... into it, ha ha. It's like the King James Bible."

"Have you surprised him with what you know? Have you impressed him?"

"I have."

"Good. Is there any milk in the fridge?"

"Yes, you bought it."

"So, it was from a good dairy? Run properly? Care taken for the calves and their mothers?"

"Ja, ja, you looked into it."

She got up and went to the fridge. "I can't remember everything. Too much has happened too fast on this island."

It came in bottles that still had the cream on top. She poured herself a glass and leaned against the counter in her jeans and black hoodie that had the Boston Bruins B in golden yellow. In a moment, she had a cream mustache. She knew she did and didn't wipe it away. She never had since I'd known her as a ten-year-old.

"To my own self be true, hmm?" she murmured.

"That's what Bill said." I ate another piece of the apple I'd pared.

"So, I can listen to the happy English worship songs on YouTube. Sing them. I can teach myself guitar and play them. That can be part of my new faith, ja? To my own self be true?"

"Ja."

"Stop saying ja. Can't we get away from all that?"

"You say it all the time."

"We both need to stop," Eve insisted. "I want to be an island girl like Jazz and Issime and Kara. Sort of."

I felt my thick dark eyebrows come together. "Sort of?"

"I want my own style. My own beliefs. I want to be new."

"So, seeing me read that nasty old Martin Luther's Bible isn't going to drive you crazy?"

"I won't even notice. I'll be reading my new English Bible. The words actually sound like the way you and I talk. The way everyone talks."

"Well, maybe you'll read some of it to me." I shrugged.

She looked at me. "Instead of Martin?"

"I can read him on my own. When I'm in one of my Amish moods."

"Okay, so well, good ... cool ... where would you like me to start?"

"The Sermon on the Mount in Matthew. Then the Psalms."

"It's on my bed. I'll just fetch it ... get it ... grab it ..."

"Why are you using so many words?" I asked.

"I'm trying to find the best ones," she told me.

"There was a time I thought you might want to speak Pennsylvania Dutch with me."

"Absolutely not."

"I get that."

Eve laughed. "*Gut*. We just sounded like Jazz and Issime."

"Ha ha. Except for the *gut*."

"Did I do that? No."

"You did it."

"God must help me."

Eve: You see how relaxing a translation it is?

Me: Yes. It's good. But that doesn't change the hard passages into soft ones. You still have to figure things out.

Eve: Well, that's what you have a brain and a heart for. And a spirit.

ME: AND TEACHERS AND PASTORS AND BISHOPS.

EVE: MAYBE. IT'S ALWAYS GOOD TO LISTEN. BUT YOU STILL HAVE TO MAKE UP YOUR OWN MIND.

ME: WHAT?

EVE: WHAT *WHAT*? WHEN YOU HEAR A MESSAGE AT CHURCH DON'T YOU CONSIDER WHETHER YOU AGREE WITH ALL OF IT OR NOT? SO, RIGHT AWAY, YOU ARE DECIDING WHAT TO KEEP AND WHAT TO SHELVE. IT IS ALL OPINION, DENNA. I DON'T CARE HOW GOOD A PASTOR OR A TEACHER OR A FRIEND IS. UNLESS THEY ARE GOD IT IS JUST THEIR OPINIONS YOU ARE HEARING.

ME: UNLESS THEY ARE A PROPHET.

EVE: YOU STILL HAVE TO COME TO SOME SORT OF UNDERSTANDING OF WHAT'S BEEN SPOKEN, JA? YOU HAVE TO INTERPRET. AND THAT IS YOU MAKING A CHOICE AND HAVING AN OPINION. EVERY PERSON WHO TALKS TO US ABOUT ANYTHING SPIRITUAL IS OFFERING AN OPINION TOO. THEY CANNOT PROVE ANYTHING. IT'S ALL CONJECTURE, ISN'T IT? THAT'S WHY THERE ARE SO MANY DIFFERENT RELIGIONS. CAN YOU COUNT THEM ALL?

ME: OKAY, OKAY. EVE, THE THINKER.

EVE: YOU SOUND LIKE MY UNCLE ZADOK. *DON'T GIVE THE GIRL A BOOK. IT WILL ONLY COMPLICATE THINGS AND PUT IDEAS IN HER HEAD.*

ME: WELL, YOU ARE COMPLICATED.

EVE: OH, I'M BURSTING AT THE SEAMS! I'M SO GLAD I HAVE SOMEONE TO TALK TO AGAIN.

ME: I FEEL LIKE YOU'VE PLANTED ME ASTRIDE A BLACK STALLION ON A VERY FAST MERRY-GO-ROUND.

EVE: LISTEN TO ME, I'M STILL BURSTING. THE BAPTISTS SAY THEY HAVE THE RIGHT TEACHING, JA? THE PENTECOSTALS SAY NO, THEY HAVE THE RIGHT TEACHING, THE ORTHODOX SAY NOT SO, THEIR WAY IS THE WAY. THE BUDDHISTS SAY THAT ABOUT THEMSELVES. THE MUSLIMS. THE HINDUS. THE SIKHS. THE JEWS. THE MARXISTS. THE ATHEISTS. THERE'S NO END TO IT, IS THERE? THEY CAN'T ALL BE RIGHT. AND NONE OF THEM CAN PROVE A THING. IT'S ALL JUST THEIR IDEAS, THEIR THOUGHTS, WHAT THEY LIKE AND THINK IS RIGHT.

ME: YOUR RANT IS MAKING MY HEAD SPIN. YOU'VE HAD TOO MANY RANTS SINCE YOU'VE ARRIVED ON ST. SILVAN'S.

EVE: WELL, THINKING OUT LOUD MAKES MY HEART SPIN. IT MAKES ME HAPPY.

ME: I'M LEFT FEELING CONFUSED AND TORMENTED ABOUT ALL THE DIFFERENT IDEAS ABOUT GOD AND YOU'RE DANCING ON THE SHORE?

EVE: SURE, BECAUSE THE AMISH ARE THE SAME AS EVERYONE ELSE. LOOK AT ALL OUR DIFFERENT CHURCHES AND ORDNUNGS. COVERED BUGGIES OR UNCOVERED BUGGIES. BLACK BUGGIES OR YELLOW BUGGIES. RUBBER TIRES OR STEEL RIMS. CELL PHONES OR NO CELL PHONES. ON AND ON IT GOES OVER THE SILLIEST THINGS. YOU'D THINK THE WRONG COLOR DRESS WOULD SEND A WOMAN TO HELL. SO, YOU UNDERSTAND, DENNA? IT'S ALL CHOICES AND OPINIONS AND IDEAS. EACH GROUP THINKS THEIR WAY OR THEIR TEACHING IS IT. SET IN STONE. BUT IT'S ALL CONJECTURE. ALL THEORY. I'M FREE TO JUDGE FOR MYSELF. THIS AMISH OR THAT AMISH OR NO AMISH. I'M ABSOLUTELY FREE TO CHOOSE. WHO KNOWS WHO IS RIGHT OR OFF TRACK?

ME: GOD KNOWS.

EVE: BUT GOD HAS SET IT UP SO THAT NO ONE KNOWS FOR SURE. IT'S A FAITH THING, JA? A FAITH THING FOR EVERYONE IN THE WORLD. TRUSTING IN WHAT IS UNSEEN. TRUSTING IN WHAT YOU BELIEVE BUT CANNOT KNOW FOR SURE. YOU WROTE ME THAT YOURSELF.

ME: WHO HAVE YOU BEEN READING BESIDES ME? YOUR FRIEND CALVIN WOULD HIT THE ROOF TO HEAR THIS TALK.

EVE: OH, CALVIN. *PFFFT*. HIS WAY OR THE HIGHWAY. JUST LIKE EVERYONE ELSE. HE GIVES US ELECTION AND PREDESTINATION. PREDESTINED TO HELL AND PREDESTINED TO HEAVEN AND NOTHING AT ALL TO DO WITH HOW A PERSON ACTS OR THINKS OR FEELS. NO FREE WILL. YOU SEE? THEY TRAP THEMSELVES IN THEIR IDEAS AND THEN THEY TRAP EVERYONE ELSE IN THERE WITH THEM. WHY CAN'T IT BE LIKE *PILGRIM'S PROGRESS*?

ME: *PILGRIM'S PROGRESS* NOW? WHAT DID YOU DO? READ THE WHOLE LIBRARY? HOW DID YOU SNEAK THE BOOKS BACK INTO YOUR HOUSE?

EVE: I SNUCK THEM INTO THE BARN SO THERE WOULDN'T BE A FUSS. MOTHER KNEW ANYWAYS. SO, *PILGRIM'S PROGRESS* BY THE BAPTIST BUNYAN, JA? IT'S RIGHT IN THE STORY. PILGRIM IS TRYING TO REACH HEAVEN. HE FINALLY GOES THROUGH AN ARCHWAY THAT REPRESENTS REDEMPTION. "WHOSEVER WILL MAY COME" AND "CHOSEN IN ME BEFORE THE FOUNDATION OF THE WORLD" ARE BOTH ON DIFFERENT SIDES OF THE SAME ARCHWAY, BOTH IN THE SAME SENTENCE, BOTH IN THE SAME HEART, BOTH IN THE SAME GOD. BUT THE REFORMERS WON'T ACCEPT THAT. FOR THEM IT'S EITHER OR. INSTEAD OF BOTH AND. CALVIN'S MUSTY OLD BOOK. REMEMBER WE FOUND A COPY IN THE ATTIC FROM 1799? IT SHOULD BE CALLED *OPINIONS OF THE CHRISTIAN RELIGION*.

BECAUSE THAT'S ALL IT IS. THEORIES AND OPINIONS AND MEDIEVAL RUMINATIONS. BUT PEOPLE TREAT HIS THOUGHTS AS IF THEY'RE A GOD. LIKE THEY'RE SOME KIND OF ULTIMATE TRUTH. RIGHT? WELL, THEY AREN'T. NO MAN'S OR WOMAN'S THOUGHTS EVER ARE.

ME: AND THAT'S THE FINAL WORD?

EVE: THAT'S MY FINAL OPINION. SO FAR.

ME: WELL, YOU CAN'T PROVE YOU'RE RIGHT.

EVE: NEITHER CAN THEY. NEITHER CAN CALVIN OR LUTHER OR THE POPE OR THE DALI LAMA. NEITHER CAN TEN THOUSAND AMISH. OR A HUNDRED MILLION CHRISTIANS. OR EIGHT BILLION HUMAN BEINGS. WE WALK BY FAITH NOT BY SIGHT. ALL OF US. ALWAYS. YOU AND ME IN THIS COZY LITTLE COTTAGE TOO. ALL WINTER LONG.

I'm Not Here

Eve's furious intensity was unexpected. It was as if she'd been shaken and opened and came foaming out, fizzing and bubbling and spilling all over the place. Yes, Lyyndenna was well aware Eve had always asked a lot of questions. Always came up with ideas that drove her parents and the Amish crazy. Always found books everywhere and read them all, no matter what they were. She didn't just bristle with a beautiful figure and a beautiful face that meant Amish boys were always begging to court her. She bristled with intelligence and passion and a thirst to think, a thirst to explore, a thirst to say everything she discovered out loud.

But now? Now she was a barn fire. A haystack blazing away and inextinguishable. A volcano on Big Island, Hawaii, exploding with ferocity. Light and color and power and fire. And beauty. She was never so lovely as when she was animated.

It might be celery sticks with peanut butter or Cheez Whiz. Milk and a milk mustache. Deliberately walking close enough to the waves to get her long silver hair wet and shiny. Laughing with plenty of vigor at Breakers or Inked or the condo at Compass Rose or the beach at White Shell. Or singing on the lantern deck of the lighthouse. But she was more and more uninhibited and spoke energetically about every topic that came to mind. She had never been this much of a Roman Candle in Pennsylvania among the Amish, no matter how kind they were or how they indulged her. Now, Lyyndenna felt like she had a tiger by the tail. That her friend was a string of firecrackers going off and bouncing around. *Snap snap snap snap!*

But it helped. Eve did not have all the answers. Most of the time she didn't have any answers. She knew how to crawl into tight dark places and look for things that mattered there. Lyyndenna crawled into those spaces behind her and found what she'd never known existed. So that gradually she began to breathe again. Truly breathe.

Chapter 15 — Storm Surge

It never occurred to me that Eve would change her name like I did or take an interest in writing like I had-- yet, why wouldn't she? Carmina Eve sounded just that much better than Eve Mueller (which admittedly wasn't so bad) while the woman who read and thought thoughts till her brain exploded out of her mouth in a torrent of articulation would naturally explore blogging as a way of expressing herself to the world. She begged me to introduce her to Fwanya at *Spindrift* who heard her out. Then told her to submit something that connected the sea to faith and spirituality but not in any kind of dogmatic or religious way. "Metaphor things," she said he said, "give me metaphor things. Aren't you the Eve who moved in with Denna?"

"Yes, I am," she'd told him.

"So, now you're Carmina?"

"I am her, I'm Carmina. Just a pen name."

"Any Spanish blood?"

"No."

"Perfect. It's a great pen name. Give me something, Carmina, give me something *excellenté*."

So, she came up with this:

The tight whorls of a shell in my palm.

We are woven tightly in our own worlds. In our own words. In our own lives.

Sometimes too tightly. Sometimes it doesn't make us stronger or more beautiful but more fragile.

But here the shell is just right. The sea and sun and swells and storms have put in all the lines and put them where they need to be. The pattern is the pattern needed. It is beautiful to us. But to the shell essential.

What was within the shell is gone. What remains, remains important.

All that comes together is important.

All that comes together in us.

All the lines.

All the sun and sea and swells.

All the sand and sky and storms.

All the patterns.

What we lose is lost and had its time with and within us.

What remains, remains important.

Let the weaving weave.

I was there when Fwanya wanted to talk to her about it.

"You wrote this yourself, Carmina?" he asked as we sat across from him at his desk.

"Yes," she replied, a little intimidated I could see, shrinking into her chair, which was surprising.

"Denna didn't write parts for you?"

"No."

"It's a little like a chant. An interesting effect. You didn't want to add a line or two?"

"I thought about it but I scratched them out. As much as you can scratch on an iPad."

"Something like: *Don't let it weave so tightly you break*?"

"I thought about the breaking, but no."

"Why not?"

"Any more chiseling would deface it. Any more paint would smear the image. Any more pencil or charcoal would add a line too many. It's in perfect suspension right now."

We both stared at her.

"What have you been reading?" asked Fwanya. "I thought you were Amish like Denna."

She sat there in her faded jeans and white T and sandals and grinned. Plus, she was getting freckles, and how was she getting freckles in February?

"I was," she replied. "But even then, I read a lot."

"And now you're reading about--?"

"Michelangelo. So, do you want my piece or not?"

The real Eve Mueller was back.

"I do. We used to be a weekly. Now we publish every day but Monday. *Spindrift* has an enviable reputation. Our stuff gets picked up by media in Boston, New York, and Philadelphia. We'll give you a Sunday slot and see how you do. Two hundred bucks."

"Oh, cool."

I rolled my eyes.

"Can I mention God?" she asked him.

Fwanya gave her his hard dude look--as Jazz would put it. "What for?"

"Well, it's spirituality stuff, right? So, lots of spirituality people think about God, you know, in different ways. Maybe even you."

"I'm an atheist."

"So, you think about God in a different way."

"Yeah, in a not think way. Hmm. I guess it would depend how you used it. No Jesus. No Moses. No Allah."

"Okay."

"Make sure I get your stuff by Friday mornings for Sunday," Fwanya insisted.

Eve nodded. "Okay."

"And stay like this. Nothing corny or dead or fizzy."

"Nope. Even Amish, I couldn't do that."

"I'm not going to tell you what to write but the next piece needs to be about winter waves and another piece needs to be about gulls. That's all I'm asking."

"Winter waves. Gulls."

"If we get good numbers on you, then I'll give you a second spot. Especially if Big City likes you."

"Romans font, twelve point?" Eve asked.

Fwanya lifted a pen. "New Times Roman, twelve point. Go away and write and hostess at Breakers and walk the shoreline. That is all."

He smiled his smile. He only had one of them.

So, the pair of us, Carmina Eve Mueller and Lyyndenna Sara Patrick went for a walk at Northwest Beach, the one that looked west across Massachusetts Bay to Gloucester.

"What?" I asked her.

"What *what*?" she responded.

"Michelangelo?"

"Why not? He believed in God."

"The other day it was Martin Luther's Bible."

"That's settled so far as I'm concerned. I've moved on."

"To the Sistine Chapel?" I pushed.

"Ha," she snorted. "You talk about me. How come you know so much stuff?"

"I can read too."

"Ja, I'd like to know what."

"And I'd like to know what you're planning."

She picked up a stray seashell. There weren't many on this beach. "I'm not planning anything. You know in the Bible where Paul goes to Athens and he doesn't preach so much, but he still talks about God? So that's all I want to do. These spirituality blogs where I can talk about ocean waves and coastlines and horizons--let people see a good God behind all of it, and if they want to explore God further it's up to them."

"Just your opinions, of course." I thought I'd get that in.

She tossed the shell from one hand to the other. "My beliefs, my opinions, yep."

"Hawthorne and I play this game. In Romans, it says you can tell what God is like from what God has made. So, what does rock say about God?"

"What? Rock? God is strong, I guess."

"A starry night sky."

"A starry night sky? God is eternal, God is forever."

"Sunrise."

"God is light. God is beauty."

"So," I said, "maybe some of your spirituality things can run along those lines."

She laughed her small laugh. "Ha. Maybe."

When I'd first come to the island, it was the sea and shore and sky that had spoken to me about being set free and about God. I felt God was reaching out and touching me. Touching me through all the things God had made. I'd danced alone on the beach, waded into the breakers, prayed out loud in German, sung in the night.

I'd lost that. For a while. I began to regain it when the bishop showed up from Pennsylvania. Not because he brought it with him. But because his coming pushed me to recover it. Now with Eve, with Carmina, it came rushing back like high tide or a storm surge. She was like I had been the year before. She had wings. And she pulled me into the sky with her and when we fell, we plunged deep into the winter sea and emerged alive, baptized.

It was all about light. Eve went into a season where it filled her eyes and soul and found its way into everything she wrote. God was light so the sea was light, the sky was light, the air, the bushes and trees, the gulls and hawks, the curling waves and pounding breakers and the lonely stretches of sand and stones. And if God was light then it meant Jesus was light too because Jesus was God and God's face--his nose, his eyes, his jaw, his mouth, his skin--it was all God and it was all light. Even the storm was light. It was rich with light. The storm healed. Because it was God's storm.

"Well," announced Eve at our kitchen table munching her peanut butter celery sticks, "Fwanya hasn't said no to anything yet."

I sat down with a turmeric tea in a cup that had the BREAKERS logo on it. "Not even to the time you mentioned Jesus."

She smiled, drank from a glass of milk, and got her mustache. "One time, he told me. One time only. It can never happen again. That's okay. I can bring the face of God into it as much as I want. No restrictions there. Same thing."

We were both writing twice a week now with Fwanya hinting the popularity of our work was edging us towards three spots. He told me my writing had always been good but that something had made it spike. He recognized that Eve's exuberance would be part of that but not all. What else was happening?

I was sitting across from him at his desk. "I'm not sure."

"There seems to be more ... peace. As if you are sure of yourself. More at home inside your skin. Is it true?"

"Maybe."

"You've never been explicit, but your blogs have referred to some real pain in your past. And that you've undergone an identity change since you arrived on St. Silvan's. Which is almost a year ago now. I suspect it involved a lot more than your changing your name."

"It's a sea change."

"It's a what?"

"A sea change into something rich and strange. Shakespeare."

"So, now the Amish are quoting Shakespeare at me?"

"I ... I think some healing has gotten inside me, Fwanya. Made its way past my strategies and schemes and my ... clever barricades. All the obstacles and stone walls I felt were insurmountable and impenetrable."

"And you've accepted that healing? Even though it's an intruder?"

"I have. It's not complete but it's strong. It ... has a lamp."

"Why don't you tell your readers about it?"

Denna's Blog

Flood tide and storm surge carry the sea much farther onto the shore. They carry it far up onto dry land and grass and the walls of homes. We may not want it. We may fret at the damage it causes. But it breaks some things down that need to be broken down and brings water, even if it's saltwater, to what is desperate for moisture of any kind. It brings light as it glistens among the roots of timothy and mulberry.

It is rough and strong at first. Perhaps too strong. But too strong can sometimes do what anything less cannot.

Eventually it softens and settles. It brings its own form of love. It brings its own form of healing. Even if you are left with a huge part of a broken heart and eyes that still cannot see moon or sun or constellations or where sky and sea meet and part.

Chapter 16 – The Bishop of St. Silvan's

I did not expect our February 28th birthday party (for February 29th) to open the cottage door to Homesick Chick (what Jazz called the mood that came over Carmina Eve and me) and let her hang around, unwelcome, and take up the spare bedroom, but that is what happened. She acted like she was doing us a favor by refusing to let Carmina Eve Mueller or I forget our roots, meanwhile helping herself to our happiness and freedom and drinking up all our coffee and non-homogenized milk. And peanut butter celery sticks.

The problem was not our guests who arranged the celebration, who hung streamers and balloons, baked Almost Muffins, Almost Black Forest Cake and Almost Peaches Pie (the joke, because I was Almost Thirty). The problem was never Kara, or Jazz, or Kaz (our new friend the village librarian), Issime, or Hawthorne, or Fwanya, or Tyler Franklin, or his girlfriend or their crew. It was the cards that came from Amish friends and family in Pennsylvania. Well-meaning. Not intended to cut or dig in deep with their fingernails. But that is what happened.

The cards actually arrived all week up until the party. Carmina Eve or I never opened them until March 1st, a gray, sleety day. We thought it would be a lark. Both of us got into leftover Black Forest Cake with whipped cream, eating happily away while we opened the cards, most of which were written in *Deutsch*. We read stuff out loud to each other and smiled and laughed. Eve was feeling good being twenty-five and I was feeling just as good being twenty-nine. Then we went for a walk in the wind along White Shell. And instead of skipping and dancing along the deserted shore, we wound up brooding and taking on the color of the sky.

"I don't want the *ordnungs*, or Martin Luther's Bible. Or the hymns from Europe, and I absolutely don't want to marry Amish," Eve muttered as we walked together, heads bent, hands thrust in the pockets of our pea coats. "But they always set a place for me at the table, always indulged what they considered eccentricities they prayed I'd grow out of, always said things like, *God loves you, the Lord Jesus loves you, we love you.* I used to roll my eyes. I wish I could hear them say that now."

"I know. What's changed for us?"

"We don't have family here in Massachusetts Bay."

"I hardly have any family back in Pennsylvania."

"Our church was family."

"Ja, but we have family here now," I argued.

"Not blood family," she argued back.

"Blood family is fine, but some of them, well, it's just about having to put up with Aunt Rachel or Uncle Adam. They're not friends. We can't choose our family, after all. We're born into it, for better or worse. But friends? Friends we can choose. And if we draw close to them they are like family. Often enough better than blood family."

"What about the saying that family is everything?"

I can't stand that saying. "Family isn't everything. I think that's a stupid thing for people to say. Many have no family, or they've lost every member of their family, or their family has been cruel and abusive towards them. Maybe their family has shunned them, or cut them off in some way, or has abandoned them. What then? Telling such people that family is everything just makes them feel worse."

"So, what do we tell them?" she demanded.

"That love is everything," I replied. I'd thought about this a lot since I'd come to the sea. "Inclusion is everything. Kindness is everything. Grace is everything. We tell them to forget any images that have been forced into their head about a nasty hard-hearted God and give them a God who is everything."

"Ja? And what does sleet say about God?"

"You know exactly what I'm going to tell you. That God is there even in the sleet. Even in the cold. Even in the harsh. None of that stops God from being God. And God by definition is love. No love, no God. Remember? *Beloved, let us love one another. Love is of God and everyone who loves is born of God. And knows God. Whoever does not love does not know God. Because God is love.*"

"Since when did you become the Bishop of St. Silvan's?"

"No, no, I'm not wanting to be preachy, I just ... Jacob could be so unforgiving and hard ... like river ice ... as if our childlessness was something I planned in order to spite him ... and I took some comfort in God those years ... five or six years ... God's love was essential ... not just a cool thing to say, not just a heart-warming thought, not just good doctrine or something that went well with a sympathy card ... it was far more than a concept to me ... it was air ... Jazz or Issime would say it was oxygen ..."

"We all knew. I've told you that. We all prayed. But more than prayed. The men went to your husband. The bishop went time and time again. The elders went."

"Yes, of course, your father came several times, he even spoke with me, he prayed with us both. Jacob would soften for weeks, even months. He was sorry for his sharp tongue and for berating me. Yet always he returned to his old ways. He never lifted a hand or raised his voice. But the cutting words, the words that knifed into me, they were never absent long from our relationship. I have forgiven him. Months ago, by a stony beach I must show you."

"You survived, Denna. Thank God."

"I survived because I talked to God like this: *Love, draw close to me. Love, help me. Love, say something beautiful to me.* How could I share a prayer like that with the Amish? It's simply too intimate. But for myself, in private, it saved my mind, it saved my life. So, if I'm going to get homesick, all right, I will suffer through it. I won't run back to Pennsylvania and the Amish to fix my lonely heart though. Family can only do so much. Church can only do so much. I always knew I needed more inside me, and I know what it has to be."

"Yes, okay, friends can only do so much. But here is my only so much."

Eve wrapped her arms around me and gave me a hug that came with a surprising amount of strength. She didn't let go either. The wind whipped and slashed, and the sleet soaked and stung, but we clung to one another as if we were hanging onto a reef while the ship went down under us. It made me cry. I thought, *it's okay, my face is wet anyways, she won't be able to tell,* as if my tears were a deep dark secret that must never be revealed. Then I realized she could feel my shoulders heaving. When she did, she hugged me more tightly. I thought she was wonderful, and I didn't care anymore, so I let go and cried even harder.

Chapter 17 – Purple Sands

I'm Not Here

No woman is an island, no man is an island, no island is an island.

Everything is always coming at you no matter who you are or where you are. Whenever Lyyndenna went to Boston or (on the rarest rare occasion) NYC, she was always grateful she could eventually flee back to the island and its waves and white whirling gulls. But junk, remarked Kaz the Librarian, was everywhere and always followed you home.

"No island is an island," she affirmed, scanning two books for Lyyndenna. "There's always a connection to the world out there, always a causeway, always a bridge. Or, as in our case, a boat. You know that."

"Yeah, I know it," Lyyndenna replied.

"So, don't romanticize island life too much. A little of the tinted glasses is natural. Your blogs are good. So are Carmina Eve's. But more than that? It makes a person sick in the head."

"Got it."

"Like your Amish past. Right? I get the Amish romance fiction through here a lot. It's been a huge genre for almost twenty years. Some of it is good. Some of it is okay. But. But. Butty but. If the writer lays on the Amish sugar too much, the reader gags. Of course, some don't gag because they're addicted. But the discerning reader gags."

"Well, I know some of it is realistic, but some is romanticized beyond the moon and Jupiter. To be honest, no Amish I know read the books. Most of the time it's unbearable. We don't fall in love that way."

Kaz laughed. "Barns and butter churns and buggy rides. So, tell the librarian all. How do you fall in love?"

"Just the same as you do."

"Just the same as I do? I only love books. I've had my crushes, I confess. But I've sworn off all that until summer."

"Well, all right, me too then."

"You too? I thought you had a thing going with the famous author."

"I ... I ... no. No. It's a friendship. A good one. But no more than that, Kaz."

"Now here's the thing. It's the thing thing thing. I get lots of beach romance through here too."

"Beach romance?"

"Seaside romance, island romance, however you want to tag it. It's a genre too. Like Amish fiction. Like murder mysteries. Westerns. Horror. Fantasy replete with castles and dragons. So, to come full circle back to where we first began, don't make your island fiction like an ice cream cone. All sweet and smooth and drippy and melting. Don't make it so sweet and unrealistic people who know island life have to choke it down. Are you working on a novel?"

"I hadn't really thought about it." (Fake.)

"Oh, that's fake, excuse me, ha ha, but every blogger wants to write a book."

"Well, I'm ..."

"Do this thing for me, all right? Do this one thing for your hardworking local librarian. If you're going to do a fall in love by the sea thing? Because fall in love by the sea things really do happen. They do. So, if you're going to do one? Make sure it's real enough that I feel I'm right there. Right there in three dimensions. No junky junk. No cheesy cheese, the waves curled at her feet stuff or the sunset turned the hunk to gold. Okay okay, Denna? It has to be absolutely real. Or I can't be there in all my three dimensions. Truthfully there could be more than three."

"I'll do my best."

"Oh, do better than that. Please. Take this book with you too."

"It's an Amish romance. Look at the cover. Same old."

"Yeah, the chick is always gorgeous. But then. You and Eve aren't too shabby, and you're Amish so what can I say about the models they use on their covers? Put a bonnet on it and a buggy and a dude in the background. Anyways, trust me, this one's a cut above. Tell me what you think. Written by a man and wife team. Amber and Darin Arkansas. It's not a barn and butter churn story. Just let me know if it's real. Let me know if it's even just a little little real. I kinda liked it."

"Okay, Kaz, I will."

"Remember. Don't blow your shot at island fiction. Sea fiction. Beach fiction. It's important you don't do that. Because everyone on the island will read it. Don't mess it up. Cross your heart?"

"It's crossed."

"Hey." Speaking of which, Lincoln, the assistant librarian with her "midnight at sea" star-crossed looks, magically materialized at Kaz's elbow. "Is it true you're related to SG Greenwood?" Her voice was deep and resonant, which went with her dark hair and dark makeup and excessively (to Lyyndenna's mind) dark-rimmed glasses. There was even a sprinkle of dark glitter on her face though Kara had told her no one did glitter anymore.

Lyyndenna nodded. "I'm related."

"Because I just read her volume of short stories, *Purple Sands*. You know? How sand dollars look before they dry out and die?"

"I know."

"Have you read the collection?"

"Just the one story. 'Dunes.'"

"What did you think of it?" Lincoln asked me.

"It was too deep for me," I admitted. "But that was four years ago. I need to revisit it, I guess."

"It fit me just right. Now and then, you get close to her in your writing."

"I do?"

"Now and then."

"Thank you."

"You ought to spend more time there."

"Where?"

"In her head." Lincoln happened to have a library copy of *Purple Sands* in her fingers and she opened it. "*They are striking alive and they are striking dead. When they shimmer with purple blood and after the blood is gone and they are white as bone, white as gulls. Under the water they live and while they are scattered over the wet sands. But they live on display too, they live on bookshelves and on top of dressers and they live in the palm of your hand. Humans should be like this. It was what Louise had always desired for herself and for her death.*" Lincoln closed the book and smiled a white smile with her black lips and stormy black eyes. "That's how you need to write."

Kaz spoke up. "In her own way, Lincoln. In her own style."

"No. In that style. In that way. It's her DNA talking. Her blood that has a story."

Kaz rolled her eyes. "Don't be so draconian."

"I am draconian. Especially about things that matter. Like the sea at three a.m. or dark ocean swells that presage an even darker gale. This Lyyndenna Patrick here needs to leave the farm, and her intoxication with the charm of beaches and warm waves, and write about real life. About purple sand dollars and the ones that lie there drained of their blood but are still beautiful. Beautiful enough to change a woman's life. Beautiful enough to make you believe there is a god worth believing in. A strong god. A sensitive god. An artistic god. Thoughtful and contemplative. Compassionate. Complicated but accessible. Rich and colorful. A labyrinth. A maze. But still a road home. Comprehensible yet inexplicable. The god of midnight mysteries and the good sunny days of clarity. As powerful as the seven seas. A whisper like the raven's feather falling and falling and falling through a sky."

Lyyndenna didn't want to be transfixed by Lincoln, but she was. Still, she fought back against the allure of the night. "So that's your theology? That's your theory? That's all there is to God?"

Lincoln smiled, unperturbed by Lyyndenna's resistance. "Isn't that enough, Amish? Or is your god as simple as a buggy wheel or a loaf of bread?"

Kaz had moved away to help an older lady, but she glared back at Lincoln. "No to rude."

Lincoln shrugged. "I'm not trying to be rude. I just want to prod the clam out of her shell."

"She's not a sea creature."

"Yes, she is. More than she knows."

Lyyndenna's face was tight. "My God is straightforward. No, not always so simple or comprehensible. But there is a kindness even in the silence. Even in what makes no sense. Or in the cuts that have crossed my heart from one year to the next."

Lincoln turned and plucked a long dark coat off a chair. "We're going to walk. Right now. Just through the harbor and then along the sea wall. I'll start sentences and you can finish them."

Lyyndenna's face began crisscrossing with lines. "What?"

Kaz shook her head and laughed. "Lincoln and I do it all the time. But I've never seen her offer the walk and talk to a woman she barely knows. Count yourself blessed."

"Blessed?" Lyyndenna repeated the word as Lincoln, taller than her, finished wrapping a long black scarf about her throat.

"Best word," Lincoln said in her dark voice and actually grinned. "You'll see."

Becca: I thought you and I were finished.

Me: You're still part of who I am. How can we be finished?

Becca: You locked me away in a drawer.

ME: WELL, NOW I'VE UNLOCKED YOU FROM THE DRAWER, OKAY? SAY SOMETHING.

BECCA: ABOUT WHAT?

ME: IF I WERE AMISH AGAIN. IF I RETURNED TO PENNSYLVANIA. WHAT WOULD BE HAPPENING TO ME RIGHT NOW?

BECCA: I DON'T KNOW WHAT WOULD BE HAPPENING TO YOU BUT I CAN TELL YOU WHAT IS HAPPENING TO ME.

ME: YOU *ARE* ME.

BECCA: SAMUEL AND I MARRIED, OF COURSE, AND WE ARE EXPECTING OUR FIRST CHILD.

ME: WHAT? JUST LIKE THAT?

BECCA: WHAT IS SO DIFFICULT?

ME: YOU HAD TWO CHILDREN YOU LOST.

BECCA: JA, AND I WILL NEVER FORGET THEM. I KEEP THEIR BIRTHDAYS, AND I PRAY FOR THEM. I KNOW THAT SOUNDS ROMAN CATHOLIC AND NOT VERY AMISH, BUT I DO IT ANYWAYS.

ME: HOW FAR ALONG ARE YOU?

BECCA: FOUR MONTHS. AND OH, HE IS SUCH A LIVELY YOUNG MAN, HA HA. ALREADY KICKING UP HIS HEELS LIKE A FOAL.

ME: AND YOUR APPETITE?

BECCA: IT'S IMPROVED, THANK THE LORD. STILL, KEEP MUSTARD AND KETCHUP AND RELISH FAR AWAY FROM ME. AND OATMEAL. UGH.

ME: SO, THAT'S IT? POP! A TRUE LOVE. POP! A MARRIAGE. POP! A BABY BOY. POP POP POP!

BECCA: MY LIFE IS NOT RICE KRISPIES, IF THAT'S WHAT YOU MEAN. SAMUEL AND I ARE BOTH STRONG WILLED. WE BUTT HEADS. BUT I KNOW MY PLACE. AND THE WORLD IS NOT ALWAYS CLOUDY, AS YOU SEEM TO THINK. IT IS NOT ALWAYS ABOUT DISAPPOINTMENT AND UNANSWERED PRAYER AND DEAD ENDS. THERE IS MUCH SWEETNESS. MUCH LOVE. FROM ABOVE AND BETWEEN ONE PERSON AND ANOTHER. NOT JUST IN AMISH FICTION. BUT IN REAL LIFE.

I don't know why I didn't get annoyed at Lincoln's presumptuousness. (That word is too big.) But I didn't pull away. I liked her strength and confidence. I liked her stride. I liked her voice. I liked the faint smell of wood smoke and dried roses that strayed over her coat and long black hair. I liked her seriousness.

"If it were always daylight," she said as we made our way past the wharves with their perpetual smell of wood, saltwater, tar and boat fuel.

"What?" I responded.

"Finish the sentence."

"You islanders and your word games. All right. It's almost too obvious to say out loud. If it were always daylight, we'd never know there were stars."

"Not so obvious as you might think, Amish. If it were always daylight, we'd never see a sunrise. If it were always daylight, we'd only know darkness by closing our eyes, or creeping into caves and tunnels, or digging a hole in the ground and burying ourselves."

"Or by dying."

"You're assuming death is darkness. What if it's the kind of intense light that blinds you?"

"You could say *what if* about a lot of things, Lincoln."

"What color is the sea?" she asked.

I crossed my eyes. "Are we back to that?"

"Is my question too difficult for you?"

"The sea is the color of the sky."

"Always?"

"Always. Blue is blue and gray is gray and night is night."

"When is the sky green?"

I blew out a gust of breath. "So, now you've tripped me up."

"It's not about tripping you up. It's about making poetry together sentence by sentence. *The sea is the color of the sky except when it is the color of the sea. You are like the people around you until you decide to be someone different than everyone else.*"

"I feel like you've tricked me into some sort of self-discovery therapy. The kind you English like to do. Honestly, the English world is like some badly frayed or badly knotted rope hanging in the barn. It was coiled and put away neatly in November. But in April it is snarled and wound too tight to budge. So, an expert must unravel it so it can be used again."

"I don't want therapy, Amish. Though we both could use some."

"Speak for yourself." I snipped out the words.

Lincoln ignored my attitude. "Writing can be our healing. I want to write as much as you do. Maybe more. But I've only showed my notebooks to Kaz."

"Tell me again what the point of this walk is?"

"To make poetry with our sentences. To write in our heads and say it out loud. Do you want to keep walking with me or not?"

"I don't know. I do know I don't like you calling me Amish as if that's my name."

"If the grains of sand could be counted," she said.

We reached the seawall. With Hawthorne, I liked to climb up and walk it. But I hadn't been with Hawthorne for several weeks. I surprised myself by climbing it anyway. It was about nine feet high and built of large stones taken from the seashore.

"If the grains of sand could be counted," I replied, "then they'd probably be rocks."

Chapter 18 – Lincoln's Cross

By now, you are probably wondering about Hawthorne and me. Well, the beginning of the year was all about Eve and by April, with more sunshine and warm days interspersed with days of cool winds and rain, Lincoln was my preoccupation. Perhaps you see what's coming. I didn't. Even though others, including tall, dark Lincoln herself, tried to warn me. I just carried on with the flow of my high tides and low tides and was pretty happy with my new friendships, especially the incredible walks where a black-haired librarian and I drew poetry out of thin air.

> Let me make the day a blanket
> Stitched in wind and cross currents
> And the rise of fish to wings
>
> Let me wrap myself in its infinities
> Racing sliding slipping clouds
> Swift minnows in the streams
>
> Let me sleep, let me sleep
> Above the shore and the long line of sky
> Let me dream
> Let me fly

Hawthorne was forever the gentleman. I saw him on Saturdays at the Artists Group and often sat beside him when the whole crew lunched at Breakers. We talked about getting together. It never happened. I missed him but did not miss him. My days were full. After a while, I did not notice.

"So, are you and Hawthorne an off and on switch?" Jazz asked me.

I didn't get it. "What does that mean?"

"It means I can't tell if you're on or you're off."

"We're friends."

"I thought you wanted more."

"I don't. This is good."

It was Eve who pushed me on that. "What happened to all your romantic walks by the sea?"

I played dumb. "What romantic walks by the sea?"

"With the good author. That guy you couldn't stop writing me about last year."

"Mark gets me."

"He gets you? Are you Kara or Issime now?"

"He gives me space."

Eve gave me a weird look. "You are Kara and Issime now. Jazz too. With a splash of Kaz. And a double scoop of Lincoln on a waffle cone."

I sort of laughed. "Ha ha. Mock me out all you want. But he's been encouraging me to make more friends."

"And?"

"And what?"

"He doesn't say anything about you and him?"

"Of course, he does. He misses me. I miss him."

"Really?" Eve challenged me. "You miss him?"

"Sure." I made my eyes as wide as I could. "Why wouldn't I?"

"You don't act like someone who's missing anyone at all."

"I'm just busy, that's all. Blogging, my novel, my girlfriends, prayer. Hawthorne and I will connect again."

"You'll connect, will you?"

"Absolutely."

To use the lingo they all used, Lincoln got on my case too. "Do you know much about having a boyfriend, Denna?"

I laughed. "I don't know anything about having a boyfriend. I've never had one my entire life. The Amish don't do that. And I don't have one now, by the way."

"I've had a lot of boyfriends. Too many. Some good, some not so good. But this holds true for every one of them--if you want to lose them, ignore them."

"I'm not ignoring him."

"And he's not a boyfriend either, am I right?"

"Exactly."

"So, it doesn't really matter if one day he ups and disappears?"

"What does that mean?" I demanded.

"It doesn't matter to you if he leaves the island to take a job at Boston U," Lincoln explained. "It doesn't matter if he gets too busy to attend those Saturday artsy meetings you go to. It doesn't matter if he never walks a beach with you again."

"Of course, it matters."

"It doesn't matter if he starts doing those beach walks with another woman."

I had no idea what to say to that.

"Because it shouldn't matter," Lincoln pushed. "It shouldn't matter because he's not a boyfriend or man friend or love interest. Nothing romantic is going on. It's not a problem if he develops an interest in another woman. He's just a friend. Right?"

"Right," I replied pretty lamely.

We were walking beside the sea wall that stretched out from the harbor and faced Gloucester. She stopped so I stopped. Her black eyes pinned me in place.

"He's just a friend, right?" she repeated.

"Yes, yes, oh, I don't know."

"Well, you'd better know, sister. You'd better know before you end up losing him."

"How can I lose something I don't have?"

"See this cross?"

When hadn't I seen her cross? It was always at her throat. The Amish do not use such symbols, but most of the English churches do. It was a different cross though. Not a steeple cross or a glittery piece of jewelry. It looked like it had been carved out of rock.

"I see it," I told her.

"Here's the short story. I liked him. I mean, I really liked him. So, I thought the best way to handle my huge crush was to pretend I didn't have one. That way he wouldn't think I was too lost on him, too eager, and take me for granted. I thought it was a perfect plan, and that I was being so cool. Till the day he said he realized that while he was head over heels for me, it was obvious I wasn't head over heels for him. He told me it was okay. He wasn't angry just sad it hadn't worked out because he truly liked me on all levels. Before I could even respond––I didn't even know how to respond except with a *mea culpa*, to be honest––he rushed on to tell me he had been accepted at a monastery as a novitiate and would be leaving that evening. What? Who did the monk thing anymore? I began to cry and tried to explain how much I wanted a long-term relationship with him, but he thought I was just trying to make him feel good despite our breakup. He hugged me goodbye and placed his cross around my neck. It was all very fast. He didn't want to hang with me, I could see he was hurting too much, and nothing I tried to get out made any difference. It was over. Everything I said was too late."

Lincoln's eyes were wet, and I felt terrible that my situation had pushed her to relive her loss. But I also felt terrible for me. It was a premonition moment. I'm not superstitious yet I felt like her pain was about to become my pain. I texted Hawthorne immediately. Could we meet? Could we meet now?

There was no response. I found out later he'd been sailing with a friend and was out of signal range. He finally texted and said of course we could meet and that he'd been meaning to call, he had something important to discuss.

I hate that word. I hate it when someone tells me there's something we need to discuss. Never anything good comes with that word. I definitely managed to traumatize myself before he showed up at my cottage that evening, his favorite Lorenzetti pipe in his mouth. Eve said hey to him then slipped into her room. He asked if I wanted to walk.

I dreaded every step I took before I took it. I could have started the conversation but I had no idea how to do that. So, he began by saying how much he'd valued our friendship over the past year. My heart truly sank into the depths of the deep dark sea. And I was right to let it sink there.

Lincoln's story now became my story. Hawthorne was heading to Salem for the spring and summer to teach creative writing for a special program. He had decided it was time for him to form new relationships. He realized I was never going to feel the same way about him that he felt about me. It had been foolish of him to expect it. Our backgrounds were far too different. Romance was not in the cards. If he met someone in Salem, well and good, but he wanted me to know we'd always be friends.

So, then I blurted. Blurted I was sorry I hadn't spent much time with him, sorry we'd hadn't talked about exploring a closer relationship, sorry he'd be gone for the next five or six months.

But it was the Lincoln Experience. Hawthorne felt I was suddenly saying all those things to make him feel better. He assured me I didn't need to do that, gently patting me on the back, puffing his Lorenzetti and smiling his warmest I'm-your-good-buddy smile. He didn't understand my tears any more than I understood them. I only saw them as a form of liquid regret. He was on his way on the morning ferry and had to get packed. He'd be sure to text or email.

"You'll have a tremendous summer," he promised me. "All your new friends."

"Yes," I responded clumsily, trying to be brave. "All my new friends. I like my old friends too."

"As do I, as do I. We'll have a grand dinner in September. On me. At that new place, The Happy Oyster. By then you might even have your novel finished."

"Or it will be finished with me."

"Courage, Lyyndenna. You have SG Greenwood in your blood and brain."

I didn't say much more. Everything I did say was open to interpretation. Even I had several interpretations for whatever I said. He walked me back to the cottage. Half a dozen vehicles were parked in front.

"There," he said. His hug was solid. "The whole tribe's here for a visit."

Yes, the whole tribe was definitely at the cottage for a visit. I found that out once I opened the door. I should rephrase that—I found that out once what was left of me opened the door. Kara, Issime, Jazz, Kaz, Lincoln, and, of course, Eve. All eyes, no smiles.

"So?" asked Eve.

I was determined to be strong. I hadn't shed one tear with Hawthorne. I wasn't going to shed any with them. A quip was on the tip of my tongue: "Oh, it was random."

It didn't work. I stared at them. My lips quivered. I couldn't form vowels or consonants. I could hardly breathe. Tears cut into the skin of my face. I had a meltdown, and a meltdown was the last thing I'd planned.

"I'm kind of messed up inside," I finally got out. "I don't think I can fix this."

Chapter 19 — Pretty Book Covers

Losing Mark was an odd sensation. The Amish don't date and break up like the English do. They don't separate or divorce. I had not had feelings like this before. My husband Jacob had hurt me with his words, but he never left me. Only death took him. Yes, it was a choice he made, but he left everyone, he left an entire world, not just me.

It felt strange to text Mark now, so I didn't. I thought I might hear from him. Nothing appeared on my mobile. Looking for words, waiting for words, desperate for words. Why hadn't my words been enough when we were still together? Why hadn't he believed me? Why had he kept thinking I only said what I said to try and make him feel better but that I didn't really mean it? I realized what I didn't know about men or my feelings about a man I cared about could fill fifteen or twenty fat books or Bibles.

"The reason he couldn't hear you at the end," Lincoln told me as we walked the line of surf at the White Shell, "was because he'd already left. He wasn't there. His feelings had been hurt long before because the relationship obviously wasn't important to you, and he'd decided to move on. He wanted to distance himself from the hurt and the source of the hurt."

"He had to know our relationship was important to me," I replied. "We talked about everything. Especially faith. And especially writing."

"He knew that was important to you, I'm sure. Just not that he was important to you except as a conduit of fascinating ideas and concepts."

"He was more than that, Lincoln."

"Was he? And you told him so how many times?"

I went silent. There was just the rush of waves.

"Did you kiss?" she prodded me.

"Of course not!" I snapped back.

"Why of course not?"

"I don't ... Jacob didn't ... We didn't kiss much when we courted, Jacob and me. We didn't kiss much after our marriage either. He didn't seem that interested in ... physical affection. I guess our last kiss was when Daniel was born. There weren't any after we were told we couldn't have more children."

"So, this last kiss was when?"

I bent down, picked up some stones and began flicking them into the sea. "Ten years ago, I suppose. It's not like I was missing something in my life. I've never had a kiss that made me want another. I just did my duty when it was my duty to kiss."

"Your duty to kiss?"

"My marriage wasn't some sort of purple passion with a book cover and a pretty model to match. My marriage wasn't Amish fiction. It wasn't romance fiction. Just a marriage. That was Amish. With flaws."

"Amish with flaws."

"Ja. Plenty of them."

"I could just as easily say most English relationships don't have pretty book covers either. They aren't romance fiction. They aren't the Hallmark channel. They're love interests with flaws. Hispanic, Asian-American, African-American, Italian-American, Blackfoot, Lakota, Navajo, straight sex, same sex, no sex, atheist, Muslim, Jew, every relationship has its struggles."

"Some more than others," I asserted.

"Ja." She used my German. "Some more than others."

"Am I supposed to run after him to Salem and try to convince him?"

"Convince him of what?"

"That I want more. That I want a romantic relationship."

"Do you?"

"I don't know."

"Then don't. You'll just make things worse."

"They're already worse," I muttered.

"As bad as you feel about how everything's turned out, believe me, it can get uglier," she warned.

I was very much at loose ends. "So, what should I do?"

"Feel it. Hurt from it. Learn from it. Maybe he'll text you. Maybe he won't. Maybe you'll be the first to thumb a text. Maybe there won't be any texts at all and the next time you see him, another woman will be at his side. You have to be ready for that."

"I wish this were the Hallmark channel."

"The Hallmark channel is a fiction. All romance fiction is a fiction whether it's butter churns and buggies, or swords and kilts, or a misty bridge over the River Thames. Don't expect a sudden twist of fate. Get on with your blogging, write your novel, walk the seashore. Breathe."

"What about a sudden twist of faith?"

Lincoln smiled. "I've heard it happens. And not just in books, or movies, or on the Hallmark channel."

Soon after Mark had left for Salem, April winds slipped into the waves of May. It must have been two months since I'd climbed up to the lantern deck. I began to do it nightly. Eve still wouldn't touch German or Martin Luther's Bible, but I prayed in German out loud, I prayed in English, I prayed using the cool language Kara and Jazz and Issime and the others used. If nothing changed dramatically from day to day in the outside world, at least praying at night with the lighthouse cutting open the dark changed things in my inside world.

Ja, I've heard people call prayer and faith an opiate. For myself, it helped me deal with reality not as if the hard things weren't there but in such a way I felt I could get some kind of grip on them. Instead of them always having their grip on me and making me feel helpless and hopeless. That was my illusion and my delusion, someone in the artists group said. To quote Kara's response to his words when I told her—*Whatever.*

Life rushed on. The tides came in, the tides went out, the moon waxed and waned. Kara and Issime had picked up boyfriends in February and said *adios* to them by Memorial Day (a new and bewildering day for me). Jazz connected with a guy who was ten years older which made me think of Mark and myself. They were on again off again but never quite off enough for him to sail into the sunset or Jazz to lock herself in her room.

Lincoln wasn't interested in anything except psychoanalyzing me, and Kaz was looking for Miguel de Cervantes, the guy who wrote *Don Quixote.* Or maybe she was looking for Don Quixote himself. She was never quite sure. "Oh, well," she summed it up, "the book is always better than the movie."

Actually, I prayed for Lincoln to meet a guy taller and darker than her so she'd leave me alone. It didn't work. Another mystery of unanswered prayer. She came up with the idea I was so fragile I needed everyone to take turns walking with me for two weeks. This would keep me glued together. I protested but they showed up at my door, at the library, at Breakers, even at the beach, somehow being divinely directed to which beach I was on, and on what day and at what hour.

I found it annoying at first and barely disguised my irritability with Kara, Issime and Jazz who had the first three days. Kara on Monday, Issime on Tuesday, Jazz on Wednesday. However, by Thursday and Kaz, I had settled into the routine. I told Lincoln on Friday it was a nice break from my new usual without a Hawthorne. The new usual being me, myself, and I. Eve walked with me on the Saturdays though we roamed the fields around the lighthouse almost every day anyway. I probably couldn't tell you most of the things the six gals and I discussed if I tried. But I was grateful for my time alone once Sunday came around. With Daniel.

A priest or pastor or psychiatrist would say, if they were kind, that it was part of my healing. It didn't worry me that I talked with my son as if he were alive and right beside me. After all, wasn't he?

So, there were waves to count together. Seashells to collect. Rocks to gather to edge the flower beds around the cottage and about the base of the lighthouse. Crabs to examine as they scuttled. Gulls to watch as they cracked clams against the rocks. Times to snuggle and just gaze at sea and sky as if the two of us were in a forever dream.

I could swim alone whenever I wished. I knew the secret spots now. I was still afraid there were people skulking about though there never were. I was glad to be away from all that seashore skin worship. Away from being told I had beautiful sunny hair, beautiful summer eyes, a beautiful figure. I hated it if someone used the term beach body. To slip under the waves, that was the best, Speedo snug, see fish if I'd brought my mask with me, taste saltwater on my lips, watch Daniel swim as he grew older, twelve, and tall and brown from the sun and laughing, squirting seawater out of his mouth at me.

That. That was what it was all about. That was what mattered. Alone with Daniel was everything. Alone with Daniel and God.

I don't want to make it sound as if May was full of lofty thoughts of deity or prayers beyond any prayers I had ever prayed. My words and the images in my mind were quite simple really. The simplest they'd ever been. I lay on my stomach and stared at sea grass and how it rooted itself in the sand and that turned into prayer. I watched sandpipers hop and skip on the wet sand and that turned into prayer. I watched sea foam, foam. Watched suns turn white with heat, as white as moons. Watched water become vast fields of fiery gemstones. Watched my arms turn from white to tan to brown to obsidian and remembered my nickname at eleven, Inkspot.

"But ink can be any color!" I'd protested, freckles lost beneath the sun's dark work.

"Not yours!" friends and family would answer. "Everyone knows you are India ink. You can't be anything else."

All that I watched became prayer, and all the prayers I prayed wound up in my blogs. Fwanya didn't say a thing. New York, Boston, Philadelphia, and Miami media loved the spirituality I wrote, even when Jesus slipped into it, happy and confident and shining in the blue waves, and Fwanya left me alone. Now I was writing five times a week.

So, to be honest (tbh), Mark Hawthorne mattered less and less. Until he kind of disappeared like an early morning sea mist that had burned off. He was nowhere to be found on my beaches, or on my island or in my mermaid mind. Right up till his text on morning of the 4th of June.

Chapter 20 – The Next Treasure Island

HE: Hey, it has been awhile.

ME: Hey, you. Yes, it has.

HE: Too long.

ME: Right. Too long.

HE: How are you?

ME: Good good good. How about you?

HE: Never better. Listen, are you free this afternoon or evening?

ME: Free? Why?

HE: I'm coming over on the ferry. I'm bringing a friend I'd like you to meet. Actually, two friends.

ME: Two friends? Really?

HE: I'm certain you'll hit it off.

ME: You are? We haven't talked in forever, and you're sure I'll hit it off with a couple of strangers?

HE: Well, one's a colleague here and the other a student. Both are wannabe writers, so I thought I'd show them my place, show them the island and introduce them to someone who really does write.

ME: All I've done are blogs.

HE: Well received in Boston and NYC. Besides, you always said you were working on a novel.

ME: So, who are they?

HE: James has written one book and teaches writing with me. His book was a memoir of growing up in South Africa under apartheid. Luna is one of our students. Same age as you and, like you, she's working on her first novel. You're going to love her.

ME: I'm going to love her?
HE: Yes. You have so much in common.
ME: We do?
HE: You'll see. Is it a date?
ME: A date?
HE: Can we all get together?
ME: Okay. Yes. Yes, we can.

I was sitting at the side of the cottage on one of those Adirondack chairs painted a bright blue. I kind of held my phone in my hand and stared as Eve came running towards me, out for her morning jog and just finishing up. She grinned, panting, and leaned her hands on her knees as she caught her breath. She looked at my face and then made a face of her own, imitating mine. "Good morning, Miss Doom and Gloom."

"I'm not that bad," I said.

"Yes, you are. What's happened? Were you talking with somebody?"

"Oh, Mark just texted me."

"He texted you. Out of the blue. After all this time."

"He's coming over on the ferry. Has two friends he wants me to meet."

"Who are they?"

"One's a writing teacher like he is at that school in Salem. The other's one of his students."

Eve flopped down in a yellow Adirondack beside me. "Which one's the woman?"

"Who said there was a woman?"

"Which one's the woman?"

"The student."

"How old is she?"

"My age. He said."

"So, that's her?" Eve asked.

"That's her, who?" I replied.

"That's his girlfriend."

"Who said anything about girlfriends?"

"Calm down."

"I am calm! Who said anything about girlfriends?"

"Isn't that what this is all about?"

"Isn't what what is this all about?"

"He has a lady friend. He wants to show her his home on St. Silvan's. Awkward to do when he has a bit of a history with you. Suppose you run into them? Or cycle into them on your big blue machine? So, he'll introduce you to her and say she's a friend. To make it less uncomfortable, he asks a male colleague to tag along. Well, to make the meet and greet even less uncomfortable, I think I should join you."

I stared at her, face still pink from her run, bright sweatband about her head. "When did you become the expert on male-female relationships?"

"I've always been an expert."

"Always? You? Who never courted in Pennsylvania?"

"I didn't court because none of them suited me. But I understood plenty of what it was about."

"You haven't courted here either."

"I'm not going to court here, there, or anywhere."

"Or even dated," I threw in.

She shrugged with one shoulder. "None of them suit me here either."

"Huh. Maybe none of them think you suit. Have you thought of that?"

"Their loss."

"My, my, how un-Amish we are today, Eve Mueller."

"I'm not Amish anymore, so how can I be un-Amish? Anyway, are you going to take me up on my offer?"

I leaned my head back and closed my eyes. "I might as well. Ohhhh, I hate all this drama. I'm never getting involved with a man again."

"Are you sure?" Eve pushed.

"I am so sure. Just give me seashells, waves, my Bible, and my blogs, and I will be content from now on."

So, Luna, the person of interest in my drama, turned out to be very nice, very sweet, very blonde and green-eyed, absolutely unhateable, and she really did want to talk about writing. The very funny thing that happened was the five of us met at the lighthouse and walked through the dunes to White Shell. This is how the pairing fell out—Luna, in her jeans and sandals and HARVARD hoodie, glommed onto me, in my jeans and sandals and BOSTON RED SOX hoodie; Eve, in her jeans and sandals and CHEERS hoodie glommed (yes, glommed! is the right word!) onto James, fit and tanned as the yachtsmen who docked at St. Silvan's in the summer (which it turned out he was), in his jeans and boots and white AMERICA'S CUP BERMUDA 2017 hoodie (far more weathered and sun-beaten than ours were) ... and Mark trailed us all alone. That is the very funny thing.

Because that is the what I picked up on right away. He was head over heels with Luna (to use Really Old English as Jazz called it). He wanted me to like her, and he wanted us to get along. I did like her, and after an hour of nonstop chatting, it was clear we got along amazing (amazing was a Jazz-approved word). So amazing he was left out of it, following along in his khaki pants, and army boots and khaki shirt with its button-down epaulets, pipe in his hand, unlit and unsmoked, listening to Luna and I make up a storyline for a book we were going to write together called *The Next Treasure Island*. That's how well we got along. I'm pretty sure Mark didn't expect us to get along that well. Or want us to get along so well he became an accessory to the fact. But that's what happened. Eve liked her too. Ah, but Eve, Eve liked James far more. I hadn't seen her laugh like that since she was ... well, to be honest, I'd never seen her laugh like that.

By the time we wound up at Hurricane Jim's, a funky new seafood restaurant, Luna and I had plotted out half our novel and declared to each other we were serious about writing it together, me taking the even-numbered chapters and her taking the odd. Or the other way around.

The Next Treasure Island

"What makes you think this is the island Robert Louis Stevenson had in mind?" asked Fleur.

Haven sat down on a boulder and tugged off her Danner Marine Corps boot. She emptied it of seawater and sand and squinted at the jungle of coconut trees just ahead of them. "Well, I just feel that it is. Don't you?"

"No."

"You need to concentrate."

"I have concentrated. All I see in my mind's eye is a black spot."

Haven shook her head. "No. No black spot in this version."

"What makes you say that?"

"I know what happened with the black spot in RLS's take on the story and it's not going to be in mine."

"Ours."

"Okay, ours."

"So, no pirates?"

"Of course, there's pirates. Just not Black Spot Pirates."

Fleur walked up to the tree line. "What sort of pirates then?"

"Modern ones. With speedboats and machine guns."

"Why'd they bury a treasure here?"

"They were being chased."

"By who?"

"The American Navy. The British Navy. The French Navy. All the navies in the world were after them. So, they buried the treasure here."

Fleur picked up a green coconut that had fallen to the ground. "What happened to them?"

"They were shot. Most of them. The ones that surrendered were executed."

"Where?"

"Well, it had to be a country that still has the death penalty." Haven tugged off her other boot and upended it. Out came water and sand and seashells. "So, the US."

"And we found out about this treasure how?" asked Fleur.

"A boyfriend who disappeared while attending Oxford," said Haven.

"Disappeared?"

"In the stacks."

"What stacks?"

"One of their old libraries. He never showed up for classes again."

"Where is he?" Fleur wanted to know.

Haven shrugged. "God knows."

"Whose boyfriend is he?"

"Was. Whose was he."

"Whose."

"Yours."

"Mine? Since when have I had a boyfriend?"

"You do now. Or did."

"You're picking me to have the boyfriend?"

"It's fiction, Fleur, for crying out loud. It's not real. We're making it up as we go."

"So, it's fiction for us and fiction for the readers too."

"It's always fiction for us. But for the readers? Maybe not. Sometimes fiction can seem very real to them. There are definitely those who take stories far more seriously than others do. They get into an author's head and into the unreal world in their heads. Except to them it is real. Some never shake it. The characters and the story stay real to them forever. Weird, huh?"

Fleur made a face. "Weird? Maybe. But some stories do that to me too."

"Do what?" Haven stood up. "Entertain you?"

"No. Become real forever. I never forget them and the people in them are real to me too. They never go away."

Haven smiled. "You're thinking too much. This book isn't supposed to get deep like that. Unless our boat sinks. Then we go deep. Ha ha."

"I'm serious."

"So am I. We didn't script deep into this novel. So, just drop it, okay?"

"Did we script that?"

"What?"

"Them."

Haven looked where Fleur was looking.

Tall shadows were approaching them through the jungle.

Too tall to be human. Or any human either of them had ever seen.

"Was this your idea?" demanded Haven.

"I haven't had any ideas since last week," replied Fleur.

"Well, it's not my idea. I never wrote it in. And there's only the two of us."

"Didn't you tell me stories can take on a life of their own? Characters too?"

Haven stared at the jungle and her face grew tight and white and tense. She began grinding her teeth. "I did say that. It sounded like something cool to say. Something magical."

"Magical? Why magical?"

Haven shook her head and backing towards the shoreline and their boat.

But there was no boat.

She glared at Fleur. "How did we get here anyway?"

It wasn't just Luna and me.

By the time we'd finished our lobster dinner, James and Eve had made plans to go sailing. And take all of us along. These were not pie-in-the-sky plans that might happen in August or September. James was bringing a boat to St. Silvan's that weekend with a skeleton crew. (Which sounded like something out of *The Next Treasure Island*.) All of us would be expected to pitch in.

"It's not hard to learn how to raise a sail," James told us over a dessert of pecan pie and ice cream. "Or weigh anchor. Or tie a nautical knot once you've been shown how. I'm sure you all have the sea in your blood."

"What makes you say that?" I asked.

"You were drawn to an island to live. Both you and Eve. Mark too. And Linda has been sailing since she was ten."

"Where are we going to sail?"

"Just around the Bay."

"It will be a lot of fun." This from Eve, who'd never been a on a boat other than a ferry her entire life. She almost squealed that out. Almost.

"What do you think, Mark?" Luna was sitting across the table from him, glued to my right elbow. "Does it sound like a plan?"

Mark smiled a smile I didn't quite know how to interpret and sipped his coffee. "It sounds like somebody's plan."

Chapter 21— Nine Dolphins

It's one thing to be onshore looking out to sea. Another to be swimming in that sea. And to be in a large boat with an engine that cuts through the water like a knife? Something else again. A ship under sail, I found out, is different from all that and has its own spirit.

Yes, I fumbled with the lines until I got them right. Laughed along with Eve and Luna as we raised the mainsail together. Learned to feel the ship's balance and rhythm and heartbeat--there is no other word-- as James taught me how to handle the wheel of *Nine Dolphins*, to read the wind and crosswinds, the ocean swells, the movement of the hull and bow and rudder, the lift and push of the sails. Whenever I had a free moment, I scrambled up on the bowsprit and actually felt confident enough to ride it as the boat plunged and dipped (or crazy enough, according to Eve). Oh, I was delirious with a sense of space and sky and sea and freedom. Soaked, laughing, and delirious. The only one who ever joined me on the bowsprit was Luna. (Haven in our outrageously whimsical novel that I loved more and more because I felt like I was writing myself out of myself.)

There was no absence of God in any of this. Sailing, to me, was a spiritual moment, a godly thing, a matter of the soul. Whitecaps, white sails, a sleek white hull, a boiling white wake, opening the gray or green or blue water to the vivid white underneath. There was the bow spray, the hissing, the snap of the nylon of the two sails and the click of the lines against the aluminum mast, wind and saltwater on the face and hands and arms--it was all a special kind of language that I knew by heart, yet a language I knew I'd never known.

The sailing spoke of God's vastness, God's infinity, God's independence. His comprehensibility and incomprehensibility, his clarity, his simplicity, his complexity. It spoke of the endless metaphors and similes that could be applied to God and the sea and the boats that strike out over its colors of indigo, jade, and charcoal. The boat was gliding through a watercolor that was still wet—one that might never dry.

I glanced at Mark from time to time as we clipped along. If he wasn't helping sail the boat, he sat in the stern, managing to keep a pipe lit despite wind gusts and bright bursts from the waves along the hull. He watched Luna hustle about, tending to this line or that sail. I could see he was watching me too as I became a sailor and a sea sprite. I was just as fast as Luna and just as nimble if I do say so my immodest self. I never got the sense he was comparing us though. He was marveling. That's my word. He was astonished and pleased and marveling. Maybe he was composing a poem about us in his head.

We anchored in Boston Harbor and just barely rowed to one of the wharves, five being perhaps one soul too many for the ship's small boat. Ate well, took two rooms at an inn, one for James and Mark, the other for Luna, Eve and me. We girls carried on, applying Aftersun to our skin, excited about the day's sail, brushing our teeth and doing our nails.

"Did you used to go with Mark?" Luna asked me out of nowhere.

I was filing the large toenail on my left foot and didn't even look up. "What did he tell you?"

"He said you were close, that you had a good friendship, but it didn't go beyond that."

I glanced at her. Luna's face was completely open and childlike.

"That's true," I replied. "Neither of us wanted more than that."

"No romantic element at all?"

I went back to my toenail. "No. Nothing like that."

"That's what he said too. Though it surprises me."

"Why does it surprise you?"

"Because he's a handsome and fascinating dude. Kinda spills over with life. You know. Quotes and metaphors and writing talk."

"I know."

"And."

I waited, stopping my filing again. "And?"

"You, Denna. Let's be honest. You're oceans of beautiful."

At least I was past blushing or being embarrassed over compliments. "That's kind of you to say."

"Facts are facts."

I sat up. "Well, then, the fact is you're beautiful too, Luna."

"Okay, thanks, but I wasn't fishing."

"I know you weren't. You're brainy and classy and fun as well. And a talented writer. I'm sure Mark's noticed all of that."

She grinned like a fourteen-year-old. "That's how we hit it off. My third short story for him. He understood it so well, and I was impressed by that. He said he read it over three or four times and was impressed by me. So, once I'd finished the course and wasn't a student anymore, he invited me out for coffee."

I smiled at my own pleasant memories. "Yes. For coffee."

"And after many coffees, we decided, why stop now?"

I was actually okay with this. I felt Eve's eyes on me but I wasn't jealous or upset. I have to say I felt relieved.

Luna had come straight out with it all, the air had been cleared, I still wanted to be her friend and writing partner (more than ever), and it didn't matter to me that Mark was gone. Okay, maybe there was a twinge. But the truth is I hadn't really wanted to pursue it when pursuit was an option, I hadn't written him after he left and had gradually gotten used to the idea that we were not beach walking buddies anymore, and really, if Mark was going to be happy with anyone else but me, he might as well be happy with Luna. I was happy with Luna. Why couldn't he be happy with Luna too?

I'd thought Eve might interject a few comments and observations and recollections of good times past between me and Mark, very good times that did border on romance fiction and that I wasn't being honest and open about. Instead she just said she was happy for Luna, happy she and I were writing a fanciful novel together and, finally, that she thought James was amazing. I wanted more details on The Amazing James, so did Luna, but Eve drifted off with a silly smile on her face and that was that. For the immediate present.

The next day was more of the day before. Glittering wave light, sharp sun overhead, the spray from the bow that made everyone diamonds if they were splashed, winds that cut and kissed, the wheel kicking under my hands, the lines biting when I hauled up sail, the rhythm, always the rhythm and the heartbeat of a sailboat caught up with the sea, and the people on board caught up with that heartbeat and rhythm too.

Chapter 22 – Broken Shells

BECCA: THERE. YOU SEE?

ME: SEE WHAT?

BECCA: I AM HAPPILY MARRIED. I HAVE A CHILD. GOD IS NEAR. MY LIFE HAS BEEN RESTORED.

ME: SO WHAT? YOU'RE JUST A BOOK OF AMISH ROMANCE FICTION.

BECCA: I'M WHAT YOU COULD HAVE BEEN.

ME: OH, OF COURSE. EVERYTHING WOULD BE PERFECT IF I'D JUST MOVED BACK TO PENNSYLVANIA.

BECCA: YOU ARE IN A MESS IN MASSACHUSETTS. THAT WOULD NEVER HAVE HAPPENED IF YOU'D JUST RETURNED HOME WHERE YOU BELONG.

ME: SOMETIMES RETURNING HOME IS NOT THE CURE-ALL.

BECCA: IT WAS FOR ME. AND I'M YOU.

ME: YOU ARE NOT. YOU'RE A CHARACTER I THOUGHT UP. I JUST WANTED TO PLAY AROUND WITH A STORY IDEA IN MY HEAD.

BECCA: OH, THAT'S NOT TRUE. YOU WONDERED WHAT IT MIGHT BE LIKE IF YOU RETURNED TO YOUR AMISH

ROOTS. NOW YOU KNOW.

ME: I DON'T KNOW ANYTHING. YOU'RE A FANTASY. REAL LIFE ISN'T LIKE THAT.

BECCA: LIKE WHAT?

ME: LIKE YOU. EVERYTHING COMING TOGETHER. CLICK-CLICK-CLICK. IT ALL CONNECTS AND IT'S ALL PERFECT.

BECCA: IT WORKED FOR ME. IT WORKED IN MY LIFE.

ME: IT WORKED FOR YOU BECAUSE YOU'RE MAKE BELIEVE.

BECCA: I'M AS REAL AS ANYTHING ELSE YOU'RE DOING IN YOUR IMAGINATION. BLOGS, *I'M NOT HERE*, *THE NEXT TREASURE ISLAND*, YOUR PLANS FOR TOMORROW, YOUR PRAYERS, TRYING TO THINK UP WHAT YOU'RE GOING TO SAY TO MARK TO PROVE YOU'RE INDEPENDENT WHEN YOU FINALLY HAVE YOUR BIG TALK.

ME: I AM NOT SITTING AROUND THINKING ABOUT MARK.

BECCA: YES, YOU ARE. IMAGINE IF YOU HADN'T SQUANDERED YOUR OPPORTUNITIES TO GET REALLY CLOSE TO HIM LAST WINTER? YOU'D HAVE A DIFFERENT LIFE RIGHT NOW. A BETTER ONE.

ME: DRAWER! GET BACK IN THE DRAWER! NOW!

BECCA: I'M NOT IN THE DRAWER ANYMORE. I'M IN YOUR HEAD. ALL THE TIME. YOU'RE THINKING ABOUT ME AND MY AMISH LIFE EVEN THOUGH YOU'VE STOPPED WRITING *HARVEST*. YOU WONDER WHAT IT WOULD BE LIKE IF YOU RETURNED TO YOUR AMISH WORLD, AND NOW YOU DO IT WITHOUT SITTING DOWN TO WRITE MY STORY. I'M A CONSTANT, SARA. YOU'RE ALWAYS

COMPARING MY LIFE TO YOURS AND ALWAYS COMING UP SHORT.

ME: No.

BECCA: YES. I'M NOT AMISH FICTION ANYMORE. I NEVER WAS. I WAS ALWAYS YOU. AND NOW I'M PERMANENT.

ME: YOU ARE NOT. YOU ARE NOT PERMANENT MARKER. YOU'RE JUST A PASSING PHASE.

BECCA: *NEIN*. YOU'RE NOT GETTING RID OF ME. I'M STAYING. YOU'RE NOT GOD AND YOU CAN'T PLAY GOD WITH ME.

It was inevitable that Mark and I have a talk, and I suppose it was only appropriate that it be a walk and talk. Nine Dolphins anchored in the harbor and we rowed ashore precariously once again. The men took rooms at The Sloop, a B&B, and Luna moved into the cottage with Eve and I as a guest. A temporary guest did not break the only-two-residents rule. The first evening, Mark and James came by, and Mark asked if I'd like to stretch my legs. He must have spoken to Luna about it because there was no reaction from her. And, so far as it went, I knew Mark and I had to have a chat sooner or later, so it might as well be now. We made our familiar way through the dunes and onto the White Shell.

"I'm glad you and Luna are getting along so well," he said as we stood on the beach.

"That's not hard, you know," I replied. "She's a very sweet woman. And fun to write with."

"It's ... it's not the same as it was with you and me."

"No?"

"Somehow it was easier with you. I mean, easier just to talk and say everything. I find I'm less open with Luna, less comfortable sharing everything. Of course, it has only been about six weeks."

I didn't know what to say to that so I just started pitching stones into the sea, as if Daniel were beside me and not Mark.

"I think," he went on, staring out over the water, "I made some sort of mistake with you. That I hurt you or bored you and pushed you away. I'm afraid of doing that again with Luna so I'm overcautious. Even timid."

I shook my head. "It's not that, Mark. It was never that. Please don't beat yourself up. I mean it. I loved spending time with you. You always treated me right and treated me with respect. I ... I ... just never encouraged you to ... take it to a place where I accepted flowers from you, or pretty cards that gushed a bit, or chocolates or gifts ... I didn't know where to go with you, and I had no idea if I wanted romance or not. I don't even know today what romance looks like on me. I never had any with my husband, not really, so I was in an awkward place with you—the first man I'd spent any time with since Jacob. The first man who held me in his arms and made me feel so ... cherished. I should have taken it further, Mark. I should have asked for something more. But I was afraid and unsure, and I let time slip away while I tried to figure it all out. And then you slipped away."

"I wish I had done more. I wish I'd said more."

"It was up to me to say more. I didn't know how. And I didn't know if I wanted to say more. I didn't know if I wanted to go farther along the shore with you. I really didn't. You took it to mean indifference and disinterest. That wasn't true. But I never explained. I never told you about the battle inside me between wanting you and wanting no one and nothing. I couldn't even tell you when you said goodbye. I couldn't hang onto you. I couldn't tell you that I cared for you. I was lost. Now you're with Luna. I want you to be with Luna. I want to be with Luna. I hope we can make it work, the three of us, I hope we can make the friendship work."

Mark nodded and offered me a sad kind of smile. "I'll try. I'll try harder this time."

"You tried hard enough last time," I replied. "Now I'll try to catch up. Luna is a wonderful woman for you, Mark. A wonderful woman."

"Thank you, Denna." He hesitated. "So are you."

He left me on the beach and made his way back to the lighthouse and the cottage and Luna. I just had the sea and my dreams and my regrets. My dreams? My broken dreams. Like broken shells.

I had my dreams like broken shells
I could not piece dreams or shells together again
And what would it matter if I could
Nothing ever looks the same
After it's been broken once

I prayed a while. Thought a while. Wandered along the beach. It was warm, and I took my jean jacket off. I squinted at the waves and at the horizon. It was all so bright. Like steel on fire. Like sun. Like moon. Like winter stars. Winter stars in summer.

I bent down and picked up two halves of shell. A beautiful shell. It would have been perfect. I placed the two halves together. They fit as if there had never been a break. Except you could see the fine line where they had once been one. With a glue that dried clear you might miss the line.

Unless you were the person who'd found the broken halves and bonded them back together. You'd always know. Others might look and say, "Oh, it's perfect. What a great find." But you'd know. You'd always know.

Part Three (July—December)

Chapter 23 – The Kennedys

There was a beach I hadn't spent much time at called Humboldt's. It was at the northwest tip of the island and had a warm current Kara and her crew named the Zinger that could really move you along and give you a great ride on a paddle board or surfboard. It could also sweep you out to sea if you didn't paddle back to shore as soon as you came under the high cliffs, which on the maps were labeled the Kennedys. Kara called one Jack and the other Bobby. She said the Kennedy family had a small cottage on the island that looked so ordinary no one ever noticed it. If true, I never noticed it either.

It didn't become obvious to me right away why I began spending so much time at Humboldt's. I thought it was because I admired the cliffs and loved the surf. The beach, though small, was flat and white and the sand as fine as stardust. If I wasn't in the water, I read books and scribbled on notepads with pens. Or hiked up to the top of the cliffs and wandered over the fields behind it that were considered too rocky for development. (Besides, there were bylaws in place that kept parts of the island in a wild state in *perpetuity*, Daz's million-dollar word, and this was one of those places.)

"So, this has become your new go-to place?"

Jazz was lying beside me in a place out of sight but full of light where I could sunbathe in my Speedo without attracting any attention whatsoever.

I was lying on my back with my arm over my eyes. "Has it?"

"Well, when was the last time you hung out at White Shell? Or Northwest?"

"I don't know."

"I've been with you here, ummm, about seven times the last two weeks. Maybe eight."

"Okay."

"So ..."

"I like the Zinger." My new surfboard was right next to me. "I like the cliffs. I like hiking around behind them. I like the small beach. Not as many people come here and I guess I like that too. There's more seclusion."

"Yeah? You think that's it?"

I raised my arm off my eyes and squinted at her. "What are you getting at?"

"What does that mean?"

"I'm just curious, Denna."

"All the other beaches have Mark Hawthorne written all over them. But Humboldt's? He's never been here with you, has he?"

"Luna has been here several times. We've worked on our, umm, experimental novel at Humboldt's several times right at this spot."

"But Mark's never been here with her, has he?" Jazz prodded.

"No, she usually comes on her own," I said.

"Do you ask her out to come on her own?"

"I ask her to come so we can work on our book together rather than sending emails all the time. What's this interrogation all about, Jazz?"

"We were all wondering how you were going to solve the Mark thing."

"The Mark thing?"

"You're friends with his woman. You're not the woman now. We were wondering what you were going to do with him."

"I'm not going to do anything with him. He's not mine to do anything with. If Luna wants him to tag along with her to Humboldt's or the Kennedys, I don't care. I'd welcome him."

"Yeah, but I think you'd prefer he stayed away."

I sat up. "Oh, for heaven's sake, Jazz. I'm sure he's been to this beach before. He was living on the island before I was."

She shrugged, fished a green apple out of her bag, and bit into it. "He's never been here with you."

"No, he's never been here with me, and you know what? He never will be here just with me. It doesn't matter anymore."

"He doesn't matter anymore?"

"No, exactly, he doesn't matter anymore. Except as a friend. And a friend of Luna's. We're not where we were. Old news."

"None of his ghosts are here."

"None of his ghosts are here? All right. None of his ghosts are here. No ghosts of the two of us here together either. Is that what you mean?"

"It's a clean beach, Denna. Your clean beach. You're free to write whatever you want on it. It has no memories for you."

I lay back down and stared at the sapphire July sky. "I suppose not."

HAWTHORNE: I need to ask you something.

ME: Okay. Fire away.

HAWTHORNE: I see Luna's visits with you to the Kennedys as being girl time. Time for you two to work on your book and just be together. She asks me to join the two of you there now and then, but I'd rather not. It's not because I dislike you or I'm holding a grudge. I feel like it's a special place for you, for both of you. Am I right?

ME: I don't mind if you join her, Mark.

HAWTHORNE: But am I right?

ME: Yes. Yes, you are. I'd rather meet the two of you at White Shell if we're talking about a threesome.

Hawthorne: I don't mind a foursome. I can handle a foursome, Denna.

ME: Well, I can't. I'm not ready for a foursome. I'm not ready for another friendship with a man.

HAWTHORNE: I'm sorry to have soured things for you, Denna.

ME: You didn't sour me, Mark. You spoiled me.

That was true enough, too, though it took that texting moment for me to figure it out. I did wonder about a friendship with another man who was not like Jacob and not like Mark. What kind of man would that man be? The man that kept coming to mind was Mark. The writer, the poet, the man with a pipe, the quiet man, the man who quoted Shakespeare, the man who'd held me in the storm, the man who trusted more to faith than fate. That man. I wanted him. I wanted him back. But our lives had moved on like the surge of the sea.

Luna: I'm sorry. I didn't mean to cause any issues.

Me: You didn't cause any issues.

Luna: I should have realized you needed some spot on the island that was entirely your own. Not Mark's, not yours and Mark's. Just yours.

Me: I'm not upset. Your Mark was a perfect gentleman about it.

Luna: My Mark? Well, it doesn't seem to bother him not to be included in our little writing cabal at the Kennedy's. So, we'll leave things as they are without any further interference from Luna Hamilton. Is Wednesday good for you?

Me: It's perfect. I'll get there early and write my

blog and once you show up we'll sail to Treasure Island.

Denna's Blog

Today I saw a dead tree behind the Kennedys.

Coming up on it, it was branchless and black and without a crown. Stark but unremarkable. I have seen better stark.

I went past it about twelve paces, and something made me glance back.

On this far side of the tree, it was bathed in full light.

It was not black.

It was brown and mossy green.

There was a huge white cloud behind it. And over the cloud, the deep blue of a sky empty of moisture.

Now it didn't seem like a dead tree at all.

It seemed rustic, beautiful in its rugged way. It was a work of art. It was alive.

The only difference between the dead black tree and the living brown tree was I went twelve steps and looked back.

Sometimes it's good to move on.

Sometimes it's good to look back after we've moved on.

Sometimes things we thought were dead are far from dead. They still have life in them. They still have beauty.

Life is a matter of perspective.

"I think it's important," Luna said after I let her read my blog.

"For who?' I asked. "The author or her readers?"

"Doesn't everything we write have to be important to us before it's important to everyone else?"

"I know. Of course. I just hope you're not going to ask: *What does it mean to you?*"

"No, I'm not going to ask you to interpret it. I'm not even going to ask if it's about regret. Because there's no sense in the blog that you're writing about regret. It's a poem, really. It's a poem about discovery. The discovery of life and beauty where you thought none of that existed. We all have discoveries like that, don't we? They give us hope that we're not always too late to see what we didn't see the first or second time around."

Chapter 24– The J Word

The Next Treasure Island

Haven was whittling shavings into a circle of stones.

Fleur was sure she could get sparks by rubbing two dry sticks together.

The sunset was streaming golds and yellows and purples but they didn't walk out to the beach to look at it.

Fleur sat down and stopped rubbing. "My arms ache. What is this story supposed to be about anyway?"

"Buried treasure, of course."

"Figuratively speaking or in an actual fact?"

Haven looked up from her whittling. "What does all that mean?"

"Is there really a chest of gold and rubies?" asked Fleur. "Or is it the-treasure-is-in-your-heart-and-soul kind of story?"

"Both, I hope. I wanted it to have a spiritual side as well as a healthy splash of adventure."

"Well, I feel like we're in *Robinson Crusoe* and trying to survive. Is there buried treasure in *Robinson Crusoe*?"

"He meets someone."

"He meets someone?"

"Yeah, he meets someone."

Fleur began rubbing her sticks together again. "Who are we going to meet?"

"God," replied Haven.

"God? Really?"

"Something like that."

"Those shadows didn't turn out to be anything."

"This won't be shadows."

Fleur tossed her sticks down. "I'm going for a walk. We've barely explored this island."

"It will be dark in an hour. A fast and very total tropical dark."

"I don't care. I'm not spending the whole novel rubbing two dry sticks together."

It had not been difficult moving one hundred feet from the beach and into the jungle to set up a makeshift camp. Going farther in meant a lot more work. There were walls of bamboo. All kinds of vines. Thick growth underfoot. After half an hour, it hardly seemed worth it to either of them, but neither wanted to be the first one to say they were done. Fleur was worried about snakes. Haven wondered if there were saltwater crocodiles.

There was still enough light for them to be surprised by what they saw the moment they saw it.

A single wing airplane with floats had crashed into a lagoon on the southern side of the island.

Its silver flamed up as the sun sank into the sea with a burst.

Dolphins swam around the wreckage.

One of the monoplane's wings was deep into the lagoon but the other was thrusting into the sunset at a forty-five-degree angle.

The propeller and canopy were clear of the water.

The canopy had not shattered.

But no one was in the cockpit.

"Is anyone alive?" asked Fleur, her big eyes bright with the disappearing sun.

"I don't know," responded Haven. "I don't see a single person. I can even see tracks in the sand."

"I thought our story was taking place in the 1700s or 1800s?"

Haven shrugged and began to carefully approach the plane. "We've said it before. Once you keyboard or pen the first sentence a book has a mind of its own."

Whimsy is defined as an odd or fanciful notion, a capricious thought or plan, something playful, light, fluffy, unexpected, unusual—whimsical. Which is what our book was. And I began to suspect one of Luna's reason for wanting to write it with me, in her totally random way, was to get my mind off her relationship with Mark. Which was a nice thing for her to try to do. Eventually we found the female pilot wandering in the jungle, throwing coconuts against tree trunks to open them and get their milk and meat, completely concussed with no idea who or what she was. Yet she was able to help us repair the plane and take to the air, circling all the islands within one hundred miles and finding a landing strip and airfield on one. The calendar by the fuel tanks said 1932. So, yes, for sure, the storyline of our novel bewildered and distracted me.

I kept telling myself and others Mark was *not a big deal*, to use my new language skills, but the truth is he still was a big deal and everyone knew it long before I admitted it to myself. So, the book helped, the blogs helped, the Kennedys helped, prayer helped, wandering the island's wild places, sailing *Nine Dolphins*, even though Mark was on board, all that helped too. But I still didn't know what to do to forget him completely.

"Your feelings will continue to erode over time," Eve promised me. "Then one morning you'll wake up, and they won't exist at all."

"My Amish Romance Expert," I replied.

She was at the kitchen table with her celery and peanut butter. "Ex-Amish. A woman doesn't need to date every man in the country to know what a good relationship looks like."

"Or date anyone in the country."

"And she doesn't need to date every man in the country to know what a breakup feels like, or how emotions jump all over your inner map, or how they flare up and eventually disappear."

I sat down at the table with a cup of ginger tea. "I'm staggered. I'm stunned. You really are an expert."

"Don't be sarcastic, sister. It doesn't go well with your Amish side."

"Ex-Amish."

"You still have an Amish side even if you're X."

"If I do, you do."

Eve bit into a peanut butter and celery stick. "I suppose. James says he can't see it."

I laughed. "James? So, he's an expert too? Only he's an expert on Amish women?"

"Hmm. Yet more sarcasm from the wannabe novelist and X. I don't think he tries to come off as an expert. He just holds this idea in his head that an Amish woman is modest, unassuming, meek, mild, submissive and ...

well, behind the times. He didn't say backward, but I knew what he was getting at."

"What? He thinks all that?"

"*Thought* all that."

"And you let him get away with it?"

"I said, he *thought* all that, didn't I?"

"So?"

"So, I told him what a true Amish woman was. That an Amish woman, even an X, might be modest but that did not mean she was meek or weak. She might be submissive to a point but she would not be submissive to the point of never standing up for what's right. She was not backward or behind the times--she worked within her culture and tradition and yes, her faith, to make family life and community life rich, significant and beautiful. I did not want to stay within that culture but on the outside, I continue to exhibit all the finest qualities of the Amish woman."

I rolled my eyes. "Except modesty."

She stuck out her tongue. "James understood. He also understood what I've added to the mix. That's what made him say I wasn't like the sort of Amish woman he had in his head."

"What exactly did you add to the mix?"

"I can pray differently. I can read an English translation of the Bible. I can work outside the home. I don't have to be a farmer or rancher. I can be a writer. I can run wearing a pair of shorts and still be modest. I can sail, wear a swimsuit, read books, listen to worship music with drums and electric guitars. I can think differently than most Amish think if I want. I can follow Jesus like they do or I can follow Jesus in a way they don't. Electricity? Oil lamps? I can do both. Ride a horse or drive a car? I can do both. Wear a dress or wear jeans? Makeup or soap and water? Wood stove or gas stove? Movies or look up at the stars? God grants me more freedom than the Bishop does."

"And this is who James wants?"

The faintest hint of a blush on her cheeks like a brushstroke. "*Ja.*"

Of course, the question was—why wouldn't James want to be close to a young woman like Eve? And the answer was—there is no reason he wouldn't want to be close to a young woman like Eve. No reason in heaven or on earth. There's also another answer—there is no reason Eve wouldn't want to be close to a young man like James. No reason in heaven or on earth.

I walked on top of the Kennedys alone under August's round moon a few nights later. Everything was bright. The surf churned at the foot of the cliffs as if it were white paint. I wore my jeans and denim shirt and jean jacket. And, oddly enough, a seashell on a brown leather cord Mark had given me earlier in the year. It didn't upset me to have it around my neck. It didn't bring me peace either. Still, every now and then, my hand went to my throat and I rolled the shell between my fingertips.

Eve and I had both been raised not only to walk with an Amish God but to marry and raise a family with an Amish Man under the blessing of that Amish God. Strangely enough, it hadn't bothered me to enjoy a relationship with a non-Amish Man once I got used to it. Now that it was gone, I wanted it back. Yet Eve and James being together? It got under my skin.

There was no rational reason for this. James was handsome, upbeat, optimistic, had a sunny faith and he treated Eve like royalty from one of Kaz's seaside romances: *The Princess on the Shore.* Eve, in turn, had quickly warmed up to his friendship, and July saw them spending every spare moment together. James actually roomed at Mark's house on St. Silvan's through the summer, and he and Eve walked together, beachcombed together, swam together, rockhounded, climbed the lighthouse at night (*my* lighthouse to climb, thank you) and often sailed *Nine Dolphins*. Just the pair of them on that forty-foot boat. Eve could be counted on to handle the sails. She was stronger and fitter and turning into quite the sailor. A sea dog of the seven seas. So, my problem was exactly?

KARA: YOU KNOW WHAT YOUR *PROBLEMO* IS, RIGHT?

ME: NO, I DON'T KNOW WHAT MY *PROBLEMO* IS, OR I WOULDN'T BE HERE IN YOUR CONDO TALKING TO YOU GUYS.

KARA: I THINK YOU KNOW.

ME: I DON'T KNOW.

KARA: YOU KNOW.

KAZ: OKAY, OKAY, ENOUGH OF THE QUIZ SHOW, KARA.

ISSIME: SHE'S JUST DANCING WITH YOU, DENNA. IT'S SO ONE OF THE MOST COMMON FEELINGS ANYONE CAN HAVE.

JAZZ: ANYONE.

KARA: EVEN X-AMISH.

KAZ: COME ON, DENNA. IT'S THE J WORD.

The J word was the Jealous word. I fought it. No, that was not it, not it. But yes, yes, it was. It took me ten or fifteen minutes to get there but I knew it was there inside me: *How come, God, Eve has a man and it's going so well for her?* The girls prodded me deeper and after another ten minutes, I said, *"Okay, I'm also J because Eve didn't hesitate. She went for relationship with James. No handwringing, no one-step-forward-three-steps-back, no lying awake at night and saying should I, can I. I hung back. Eve never hung back. She made a beautiful connection with James. I hung back. I lost my connection with Mark. End of story."*

KARA: IT WAS A BEAUTIFUL CONNECTION. NOT JUST A RANDOM CONNECTION. NOT A MAC 'N' CHEESE CONNECTION.

JAZZ: YEAH, IT WAS INCREDIBLE. ALL YOUR BEACH WALKS AND POETRY AND SHAKESPEARE--AMAZING.

ISSIME: THE PIPE DUDE. I ALWAYS WANTED A PIPE DUDE FOR A DATE. MAYBE MORE.

KAZ: YOU GUYS. HOW DOES THIS HELP? SHE GETS SHE'S BEEN J. NOW SHE'S BEATING HERSELF UP BECAUSE SHE HAD THE CONNECTION, SHE DIDN'T GO FOR MORE OF A CONNECTION, NOW THERE'S NO CONNECTION. AT LEAST, NOT THE R KIND. IT TOOK TOO LONG FOR HER TO REALIZE SHE WANTED THE R.

ME: IT DIDN'T TAKE EVE ANY TIME AT ALL.

JAZZ: DENNA, YOU ARE WHO YOU ARE. YOUR CHEMISTRY IS DIFFERENT. YOUR STAR SIGN IS DIFFERENT. YOUR SOUL IS NOT ON THIS PLANET. NOW YOU'VE FIGURED IT OUT. WE ALL FIGURE THINGS OUT BUT IT TAKES TIME. SO, TODAY YOU CAN GO FOR R. YOU KNOW YOU WANT R. ROMANCE. ROMANCE WILL COME TO YOU BECAUSE YOU'VE OPENED YOUR HEART.

ME: I'VE OPENED MY HEART? TO WHO?

JAZZ: TO A MAN. A MAN YOU LIKE. ANY MAN.

ME: I DON'T WANT ANY MAN.

JAZZ: THEN GO BACK TO MARK. TALK TO MARK.

ME: HOW CAN I GO BACK TO MARK? MARK IS WITH ANOTHER WOMAN. MARK IS WITH A WOMAN WHO'S MY FRIEND. I CAN'T TALK TO MARK AND SAY, *HEY, MARK, I'VE FINALLY FIGURED IT OUT. I'VE FIGURED OUT THE J AND THE R.* IT'S TOO LATE FOR MARK.

JAZZ: IT'S NEVER TOO LATE. YOU CAN TALK TO HIM. YOU CAN TALK TO HER. THEY'RE NOT MARRIED OR SOMETHING.

ME: THEY MAY NOT BE MARRIED BUT THEY DEFINITELY ARE OR SOMETHING.

LINCOLN: JUST A TALK. JUST TELL MARK WHAT YOU'VE FOUND OUT ABOUT YOURSELF.

ME: ABSOLUTELY NOT. WHAT'S WITH YOU GUYS? THEY'RE TOGETHER. MARK AND LUNA ARE TOGETHER. I'M NOT GOING TO CRASH THAT. NONE OF YOU WOULD EITHER.

LINCOLN: YOU COULD—

ME: NO. I COULDN'T. END OF STORY. IT'S END OF STORY.

Chapter 25 – The Shunning

I never knew until the second summer how exhausting a life an X might have. I should have stayed Amish, I told myself a dozen times. Things would be peaceful. Things would be orderly. Things would make sense. But now look at this. Look at this mess.

I'm Not Here

Nobody told her to do it, it was an instinctual act, but she went to Eve first, took her out for coffee at Inked and explained about her feelings of jealousy and the other R word, Regret. Eve was uncomfortable with all this opening up stuff and told Denna that. Eve almost said it was Not The Amish Way—Denna knew it was on the tip of her tongue. But after the third coffee, Eve loosened up and thanked her.

"Okay, I did feel there was a problem between us," Eve admitted. "So, thanks for clearing the air. I really can't blame you. It's hard navigating this X-Amish business. What are we supposed to feel and think and when are we supposed to think and feel it? Even with James I'm going: *Left foot, then right foot, left foot, then right foot.*"

"I'm happy for you, Eve," Denna said. "You need to know that. It's just, watching you with James, I wish I'd acted differently with Mark. I wish I'd taken some risks. I wish I'd ... I wish I'd taken him in my arms."

"Someone else will come along, Denna."

"Oh, the island is full of Someone Else's, on season and off."

Eve smiled. "You want a well-educated pipe-smoking author dude."

"Ha. You're sounding more like Kara and Jazz every day."

"So are you."

"I don't know what I want. Except I still want Mark."

"That's obvious."

Denna stared. "It is?"

"Yes. And not just to me."

"James?"

"Oh, definitely. He's mentioned it."

"Do you think ... Luna? Mark?"

"Yes."

Denna pulled out her mobile. "Then I have to meet with Luna. I have to make sure she understands where I'm coming from."

Eve nodded and sipped her cappuccino. "I agree."

"Would you have brought all this up with me if I hadn't told you what I was feeling?"

"No. I wouldn't have."

"Why not?"

"I'm still too Amish. I'm not X enough. I'd have had no idea how to broach such a subject with you except in the most awkward way. Amish don't have to talk about the things you're talking about. Not usually."

"Oh, so now the Amish we left behind are perfect. They're Amish fiction."

"No. I'm sure there were many young women who wanted the same young man and the Bishop and Elders had to deal with it. I know for sure there were two women who wanted out of their marriages, and one of them had her heart set on a single man a year younger than she was."

"How do you know that?" demanded Denna.

"I heard my father talking about it with my mother when he thought I wasn't around," Eve said. "I have no idea how it was resolved. She was still with her husband when I left and the single guy she wanted was getting engaged to someone else."

"Who? Who are they?"

"Oh, never mind. I shouldn't have told you. It just takes your mind back there. Your mind needs to be here dealing with your own imperfect world of Island Romance Fiction, ha ha. Have you texted Luna?"

"Just."

"Did she respond?"

"Just."

"So?"

"The White Shell in half an hour."

An August afternoon wind was up and coming in off the sea. Denna didn't go back to the cottage where Luna was, she went right to the beach. Luna was already there and the two women hugged, but Denna could tell Luna was not as free and upbeat as she'd always been when they got together. So, she decided to launch into it right away.

"Luna, I'm having a much harder time letting go of Mark than I thought," Denna said. "Which is not me saying I'm going to fight you for him or I want him back. It's me saying I think you're amazing and that the two of you are perfect together. It's me saying I wish I'd had the courage to seize the opportunity I had like you did. I want you to know I've learned from this, I'll meet someone else, and the next time I won't wait forever. I'll act."

Luna remained as cool as the sea. "So, that's it? That's what you wanted to tell me? That you're still after my man?"

"I'm not after your man. I still have feelings for him, apparently I can't hide that from anyone, even you, and I—"

"No," Luna snipped. "You can't."

Denna felt the heat rise in her cheeks. "I'm sorry. I didn't ask to see you to make a formal declaration of war. I'm having a hard time understanding myself and I don't often get what's going on in me before others do."

"Oh, my my my, you don't, pretty Amish girl? I expect you'll learn. Before some woman whose man you want knocks your head off your neck. Which I'm perfectly capable of doing. We've never talked about Luna the Black Belt in Shotokan Karate, have we?"

"Do we have to?"

"If you're going to get in my way, yeah."

"Get in your way?"

Luna's blue eyes were burning skies. "I'm not some dumb blonde with blonde moments. I've noticed how cute you can get around Mark. I've ignored it because I liked you and, after all, you had a past together. But now it's getting too much. You come to me like it's some sort of confessional and blurt out you want Mark to be your man. No, he's not going to be your man. Over my dead body. I don't care how many mistakes you made in your relationship with him. I don't care how difficult is to un-Amish your Amish background. Stay away from him and stay away from me. Get your life together with someone else. Not Mark Hawthorne. And not Luna Marshall."

Denna stayed at White Shell another hour before returning to her cottage.

Eve was sitting outside in one of the Adirondack chairs. "What story is on your face?"

Denna flopped down in a chair next to her. "I don't know. I really don't know anything anymore. What story is on yours?"

"Luna picked up all her stuff and moved out. James came for her in his truck."

BECCA: I'M TRULY SORRY.

ME: OH. WHAT ARE YOU DOING HERE? DID YOU POP UP SO YOU COULD GLOAT?

BECCA: WHY WOULD I WANT TO GLOAT? I'M IN YOU AND YOU'RE IN ME. WHATEVER HURTS YOU HURTS ME.

ME: IT'S A MESS. IT'S ALL A MESS. I TRIED TO DO THE RIGHT THING. BUT WHAT DO I KNOW ABOUT DOING THE RIGHT THING AS AN AMERICAN WOMAN? EVERYTHING'S WORSE THAN IT WAS TWENTY-FOUR HOURS AGO. I SHOULD HITCH A RIDE BACK TO PENNSYLVANIA.

BECCA: THAT WOULDN'T BE RETURNING IN THE RIGHT SPIRIT. YOU'D JUST BE RUNNING AWAY. YOU CAN'T COME BACK TO US LIKE THAT.

ME: I'LL GO BACK TO THE NOVEL ABOUT YOU. I'LL GO BACK TO *HARVEST.* I'LL WRITE IT IN. SARA RETURNS TO THE PENNSYLVANIA AMISH.

BECCA: YOU'RE NOT WRITING THAT STORY ANYMORE. YOU'RE NOT CAPABLE OF WRITING IT.

ME: WHY NOT?

BECCA: YOU LEFT ALL THAT FAR BEHIND. YOU'VE KEPT SOME OF IT. BUT IT'S INTERWOVEN SO TIGHTLY WITH THE DIFFERENT WOMAN YOU'RE BECOMING IT CAN'T BE SEPARATED OUT AND PUT IN A NEW YOU ALL BY ITSELF. YOU WILL HAVE TO KEEP GOING FORWARD AS YOU ARE, A MIX OF MANY THINGS. YOU CAN'T BE ME ANYMORE. YOU CAN'T JUST BE AN AMISH WOMAN. BUT I CAN REMAIN IN YOU FOR GOOD.

ME: ARE YOU SURE?

BECCA: YES, I AM. I'M IN YOUR HEART. I'M IN YOUR SOUL. OTHER THINGS ARE THERE TOO. OTHER PARTS OF YOU. BUT I'M STITCHED IN AS DEEPLY AS STITCHES CAN GO.

Nine Dolphins kept sailing but not with me on board. Luna texted me that I wasn't welcome on the boat, at Mark's home, or in her company at any time. Eve kept sailing, of course. She was James's girlfriend. She would return from her outings more tanned than ever, happiness all over her face and body, but had nothing to say to me.

Gradually, we drifted apart. There didn't seem to be anything to talk about that didn't include Luna and James and Mark. We ate at separate times and went on walks without each other. She was spending more and more time with James anyway. I walked alone or with one of the girls--Jazz, Issime, Kara, Lincoln, or Kaz. To be honest, as much as everything that was happening hurt, they were more than enough.

LINCOLN: I'VE READ A FEW AMISH FICTION BOOKS, AS YOU KNOW.

ME: RIGHT. I KNOW.

LINCOLN: MOST OF IT IS NOT TO MY TASTE. TOO SUNNY-SIDE UP.

ME: OKAY.

LINCOLN: BUT OTHERS? WELL, WHAT YOU'RE GOING THROUGH RIGHT NOW SOUNDS LIKE AN AMISH SHUNNING.

ME: EXCEPT NONE OF THEM ARE AMISH.

LINCOLN: EVE IS.

ME: X-AMISH. LIKE ME.

LINCOLN: THERE'S STILL PLENTY OF AMISH LEFT IN BOTH OF YOU FOR ALL THE WORLD TO SEE.

ME: REALLY.

LINCOLN: REALLY. AND SHE SHOULD KNOW BETTER THAN TO EXCLUDE YOU LIKE SHE'S DOING.

ME: WHY? WHY SHOULD SHE KNOW BETTER?

LINCOLN: BECAUSE OF THAT WHOLE GROUP SHE WOULD KNOW WHAT SHUNNING LOOKS LIKE. SHE WOULD KNOW WHAT IT FEELS LIKE TO BE THE PERSON WHO IS BEING SHUNNED. SHE WOULD KNOW HOW IT HURTS. AND SHE WOULD KNOW THAT SO FAR AS EVERYTHING GOES ABOUT THE AMISH FAITH, SHUNNING IS THE ONE

PRACTICE THAT IS MOST WRONG.

ME: I DON'T KNOW IF SHE WOULD KNOW ALL THAT.

LINCOLN: WHY WOULDN'T SHE KNOW ALL THAT? IT'S
THE CULTURE SHE WAS BORN AND RAISED IN.

ME: I JUST DON'T THINK SHE WOULD GO THERE. SHE
WOULD SAY I SPOKE INAPPROPRIATELY TO LUNA AND
NOW THAT I'VE MADE MY BED I HAVE TO LIE IN IT.

LINCOLN: HOW DID YOU SPEAK INAPPROPRIATELY?
SHE WAS THE ONE WHO TOLD YOU TO BE UP FRONT
WITH LUNA AND TELL HER ALL YOUR FEELINGS. NOW
SHE'S ACTING LIKE YOU DID THE WRONG THING AND
THAT SHE HAD NOTHING TO DO WITH ENCOURAGING
YOU TO OPEN YOUR MOUTH? WHAT A HYPOCRITE.

ME: HUSH.

LINCOLN: IT'S TRUE. YOU KNOW IT'S TRUE.

ME: I'VE TRIED TO BRING THE WHOLE THING UP ONCE
OR TWICE. SHE WON'T TALK ABOUT IT AND SHE WON'T
ADMIT TO ANYTHING. WE BARELY SAY TWO WORDS TO
ANOTHER AS IT IS.

LINCOLN: SO, THIS IS A GOOD THING? THIS IS A
CHRISTIAN THING? AN AMISH THING?

ME: IT'S THE THING THAT IS. I'LL HAVE TO LEARN TO
LIVE WITH IT.

Chapter 26 – Running Along the Seashore

For all we saw of each other, Eve and I might as well have been living in different cottages. I can't say the chill between us didn't bother me. That would be a lie. But a lot of things in life had already hurt and had not drowned me in the sea. I would not let this put me under the waves either.

Often the girls asked me not only how I felt about Eve's actions, but how I felt about Luna's and about how James and Mark were treating me by shutting me out of their lives. Well, some days it cut to the bone. Other days I did not think about it. A moment you'd think would have hurt the most actually blessed me.

I was at the Kennedys, right at the top edge of the cliffs, not a safe place to stand in a strong wind, when I saw *Nine Dolphins* glide past beneath my feet. I could see Mark with his arm around Luna's waist. Eve was steering the boat with James standing behind her and offering advice, hands resting on both her shoulders. I braced myself to feel the sting. It did not come.

Instead I saw the play of light on sails and hull. It sped over their wake and lit every whitecap. The sky had been overcast. Just after the sailboat moved out of sight to the northeast, the gray began to pull apart like cotton batting and sun spread through the rips and tears. The world became as luminous as stars and constellations. I sat down, hugged my knees to my chest and took it all in. I forgot about *Nine Dolphins* and its crew in moments. Especially when the gulls swooped by crying their wild cries. To me, it was God Talk: *Never mind the people on the boat. Look at my world. Look at your world. It shines. It sparkles. It bursts with life of all kinds. Be there. Stay there. Live in that world.*

Which didn't mean I promptly forgot all about the people on the boat and the pain and isolation they were inflicting on me. It also didn't mean I never prayed about them or for them ever again. But there's no question their force on my life began to diminish, and they pushed their way into my thoughts and my heart less and less. I came out of the tunnel a bit. Even Eve noticed.

"What do you have to be so happy about?" she snapped at me one morning in the kitchen.

"Not you," I snipped back.

All of us have read books or memes about bad things leading to good things, one door closing and another door opening, the darkest hour being just before dawn. I have nothing to say about that. I came to the island because I was hurting in Pennsylvania, and the island gave me room to breathe again and hope again. But then the island took that breath and hope away. It didn't give it back either. God had to do that.

I had set aside my German Bible months before. No longer sang my German hymns. Didn't pray in German much. Didn't think in German much. God came to me regardless (though one small part of me wondered if I might be punished for ignoring my Amish heritage). God came to me more beautifully than I had yet experienced. In Pennsylvania or Massachusetts.

Prayers were simpler and, I felt, far more authentic. So were my thanks and my worship. Passages in the Bible shimmered and went right to the heart, they opened up my mind and my thoughts. The island became a holy island. Everything was touched by the heavens--tall grasses, dunes, rollers, the darkening of the sun on the back of my hand. The burn of saltwater on my lips was as good as lungfuls of air that crossed the ocean from Britain and France and Ireland. Swimming was perfect and lying under the sun in my swimsuit in my secret places just as perfect.

I sang on my lighthouse deck, and the moon rose and set like a hand that blessed. Far out over the sea the light shone, warning the ships, encouraging the ships, guiding the ships. It was easy to read my English Bible up there and I thought of it as a light of guidance too, which was different for me. I'd always considered it a good book and an inspired book, but I also thought of it as a law book, a book of rules and commands and legal things, not a book where I went for a sweet kind of guidance or nurture or grace. Now it became a gentle book, a book that nudged me along. Though I was not unaware of the harsher passages, it seemed I was drawn to the breezes and meadows and summer fireflies of the Bible, to the coals that glowed in the fire pits of the long nights. There I was loved with a love I had not looked for before, a love that perhaps I had not thought I wanted, one I had not sought, but a love which overturned every rough stone, and walked every jagged shoreline, and every smooth strand of sand, and found me. I was so caught up in light I didn't need more than four hours sleep before I was up and walking again, swimming, riding my mountain bike, driving Bachi to the Kennedys, iPadding my blogs, grabbing a bite at Breakers or The Happy Oyster, running, yes, running along the seashore, running out of breath, then finding it again when I stopped, and caught it, and looked out to sea and saw everything.

Chapter 27 – God with a Face

About halfway through September, Eve moved out and began sharing a room with Luna who was at The Bristol. This was not something Eve announced ahead of time or prepared me for, though I wasn't surprised. The only surprise was coming home and finding her gone and all her stuff gone with her. Including the last jar of peanut butter and the last bag of celery. What made it stark was that she left everything Amish perfect--floors were swept, bed linen changed, the shower scrubbed, fresh flowers placed in a vase on the kitchen table. Open windows let in a crisp sea breeze. I watched the lace curtains flip and turn for a few minutes, taking it all in.

Eve had followed me here from Pennsylvania. Her parents had entrusted her into my care. I'd listened for hours as she worked her way free of the Amishness she wanted to leave behind and persisted in clinging to what she refused to relinquish. We'd walked together, beachcombed together, prayed together and, for a time, sailed together. My friends became her friends. Now she was gone. There was only the note propped against the vase of yellow flowers. *With Luna at The Bristol. Thanks for the loan of the room. God bless. Take care. Eve*

Combined with everything else, this should have wrecked me. I think the old Sara would have collapsed to her knees and wept. But I was finding spirituality in a different way than the Pennsylvania way. God was making my darkness light up like a sunrise. Like the Bible spoke it, my darkness was the sun at its zenith in his eyes. He would find a way to illuminate my life. He had already been doing that before this latest blow. So, I stood there, watching the sea breeze move the lace curtains in a lazy ocean's swell way, saw Eve's note drift to the floor and was in a mood that anticipated something strong and good coming through the door behind me. Unsurprisingly, it turned out to be Kara and the crew.

Jazz had seen James dropping Eve off at The Bristol and helping her carry in her luggage. She'd gone over and asked Eve what was up. Eve had been polite but cool and said it was time for some fresh air. Jazz had offered to help. James said he could handle it. Jazz moved on. Texted the girls. When they were all free, they piled into Kara's jeep and shot down to the cottage, Round Turn and Two Half Hitches, and barreled inside, swarming me with a group hug, pushing me into a chair and plying me with a blend of tea named after St. Silvan's.

JAZZ: THIS HAS BEEN CRAZY. IT'S ALL BEEN CRAZY. HOW ARE YOU DOING EXACTLY?

ME: EXACTLY?

JAZZ: YES. I DON'T WANT VAGUE ASSURANCES OR HUGE GENERALITIES.

ME: VAGUE ASSURANCES?

JAZZ: STOP PARROTING ME, DENNA. WE ALL WANT TO KNOW HOW YOU'RE DOING.

LINCOLN: WE CAN BE HONEST WITH YOU, RIGHT? AFTER ALL THIS TIME? ARE YOU HAVING, WELL, PANIC ATTACKS OR ANYTHING?

ISSIME: YEAH. I FIND THIS WHOLE THING DEPRESSING. AND I'M NEVER DEPRESSED. SO, IF THAT'S HOW I FEEL, HOW DO YOU FEEL? REALLY?

KARA: WE DON'T LIKE IT WHEN PEOPLE SAY THEY'RE OKAY WHEN THEY'RE NOT OKAY. IT'S BEEN MY EXPERIENCE THAT RELIGIOUS PEOPLE DO THAT A LOT. DO THEY THINK THEY HAVE TO PUT UP A GOOD FRONT FOR GOD'S SAKE? *NO, I BELIEVE IN A GOOD GOD SO I NEVER HAVE ANY TROUBLES HE CAN'T SEE ME THROUGH, I'M COOL, I'M ON IT, I'M NEVER UNDERGROUND, NEVER.*

KAZ: IT'S LIKE HAVING A ROMANCE NOVEL WHERE EVERYTHING IS UPBEAT AND SUGAR FROSTED FLAKES ALL THE TIME. A BOOK LIKE THAT WITH A STORYLINE LIKE THAT IS NAUSEATING. IT DOESN'T HELP ME GROW AT ALL. DOESN'T ENTERTAIN ME EITHER. I'D PROBABLY PITCH IT ACROSS THE LIBRARY INTO THE TAKE-ME-I'M-FREE BIN. IF THE PROTAGONIST HAS HARD TIMES, THEN I UNDERSTAND, BECAUSE THAT'S ME. THEN THE BOOK MATTERS. THEN WE HAVE SIGNIFICANCE. ARE YOU A HARD TIMES PROTAGONIST?

ME: I'M DEFINITELY A HARD TIMES PROTAGONIST.

KAZ: THANK YOU. PLEASE FINISH YOUR NOVEL SO I CAN READ IT AND REVIEW IT.

LINCOLN: WE ALL WANT TO DO THAT.

ME: WHEN I WAS IN PENNSYLVANIA, I WAS IN ENORMOUS ANGUISH FROM THE LOSS OF MY SON AND MY HUSBAND. I BROUGHT THAT ANGUISH WITH ME TO THE ISLAND. MY FIRST YEAR ON ST. SILVAN'S WAS AMAZING IN ALMOST EVERY WAY. BUT I WAS DEPRESSED, I WAS HURTING, THE CUTS WENT IN DEEP, THEY WENT FAR DOWN INTO MY HEART. YOU GUYS HELPED ME WITH THAT. MARK HELPED ME WITH THAT. EVE HELPED ME WITH THAT. THE SEA, THE WRITING,

THE SALTWATER AGAINST MY SKIN WHEN I SWAM, THE BREAKERS, IT ALL HELPED. BUT I WASN'T FREE. I'M STILL NOT FREE. THE JOURNEY IS LONG. WAY TOO LONG. IT SEEMS TO GET LONGER EVERY DAY. MARK LEAVES ME. LUNA LEAVES ME. EVE LEAVES ME. BUT SUDDENLY THERE'S MORE LIGHT THAN EVER BEFORE. ACRES OF LIGHT. OCEANS OF LIGHT. I'M INCANDESCENT.

KARA: HA. WELL, YOU DON'T NEED TO CONVINCE ME. IT LOOKS LIKE SOMEBODY STRUCK A MATCH BEHIND YOUR EYES.

LINCOLN: SO, IT'S THIS THING, RIGHT? THE DARKER YOU GET THE BRIGHTER YOU GET? THAT'S HOW IT WORKS, DOESN'T IT? IS THAT HOW THINGS ARE COMING TOGETHER?

ME: I CAN'T SAY HOW IT'S ALL GOING TO COME TOGETHER. BUT SUFFERING STITCHED UP WITH FAITH IN SOMETHING MORE, SOMETHING BIGGER, IS WHAT I GREW UP WITH. THE AMISH NEVER STOP THINKING ABOUT SUFFERING OR THE JESUS CROSS OR HOW THEY WERE PERSECUTED IN EUROPE. BUT FOR THEM, THE DARKER THE DARK, THE BRIGHTER THE LIGHT OF GOD. SO, MAYBE THAT'S WHAT'S KICKING IN NOW. I DEFINITELY KNOW I'M HAVING A SPIRITUAL ENCOUNTER I'VE NEVER HAD BEFORE. I SHOULD BE SCREAMING WITH THE PAIN, BUT INSTEAD I'M ALL LIT UP AND HAVE THESE CRAZY FEELINGS THAT GOOD IS COMING, THAT A LOT OF GOOD IS COMING TO ME.

KARA: IT'S THE UNIVERSE. THE UNIVERSE IS OPENING ITS HEART TO YOU.

ME: YES, THE UNIVERSE, THE UNIVERSE. IT'S GOD, KARA. GOD WITH A FACE. GOD WITH THIS BEAUTIFUL JESUS FACE IS OPENING HIS HEART TO ME. MORE THAN HE EVER HAS BEFORE. THAT'S THE UNIVERSE. I FEEL so safe. So free. It's unlike any place I've ever been before.

The Next Treasure Island

"I can't find Haven," I complained to the pilot. "She wandered off and I haven't seen her since."

Amelia put her hands in the pockets of her khaki overalls. "Actually, I tracked her."

"You tracked her?"

"I saw her take off in a hurry and wondered what was going on."

"What was going on?"

"It looked to me as if she thought she'd found X marks the spot. She dug at the jungle rot and the raw earth with her bare hands. I approached her and she fanged me like a lioness: *It's my treasure, not yours or Fleur's, it belongs in my pockets, get away, and keep Fleur away too.* So, I remained well back. Eventually, I walked off and returned a few hours later. You were napping back at the plane all this time. I found a very deep hole, I think she'd fetched a shovel from somewhere, who knows where, and the hole was empty. So, either there was no treasure there to begin with or she found it and carried it off."

"But we're not even on the first island. The island where the treasure was supposed to be."

"Stories often change in the middle of the plot."

"Did you track her after that?" Fleur asked.

Amelia nodded. "Till her footprints stopped. That's a mystery in and of itself. Bare feet and they just stopped. There were no more of them. I did notice there was a serious difference between her prints leading up to the hole and her prints leading away."

"What serious difference?"

"Her prints sank into the jungle floor a great deal more leading up to X marks the spot. When she walked away, she weighed less. Or had less in her hands."

"Was she carrying something when she stopped to dig up the treasure?"

"No."

"Then how could she weigh less carrying something away from the hole?" Fleur wanted to know.

Amelia shrugged. "She had less in her hands, something I couldn't see that was invisible to me? Or she had less in her heart? Who knows? This is a whimsical story you've brought on, isn't it? So, who knows what's really happening? Why don't you write it differently?"

"I don't do all the writing. Haven and I both do this story. Or we used to."

"Isn't she your writing partner anymore?"

"No."

"So, you can change anything you want?"

"I don't know. I haven't tried, really. Obviously, she just wrote her exit."

They were standing by the silver plane on a rough landing strip lined with wooden cargo boxes and the broken pieces of airplanes. There was a hangar that had no roof and one fuel pump. The fuel pump was full but no one was on the island. Pilots pumped the fuel themselves. It arrived by ship once a month. No one saw this happen, or what ship or company did it, or how the company was paid. The entire process was simply understood. Fleur understood it. So did Amelia. But neither knew why.

"Have you ever considered flying, Fleur?" Amelia asked, sitting on one of the cargo boxes.

"Not before I started this book."

"Would you consider it now since the plot has gotten away from you?"

"Gotten away from me? Is that what it looks like? Well, maybe you're right. I do feel at loose ends. Perhaps the relationship between Haven and me wasn't fifty-fifty. Perhaps she wrote more and plotted more and controlled more. It might have been more like seventy to thirty in her favor."

"Or even her eighty to your twenty. That's how it looked from the air before she had me crash."

Fleur was startled. "She had you crash?"

Amelia stared at her with Arctic blue eyes. "Did you write it in?"

"I didn't even know you were in the air. I didn't even know there was a plane."

"My point. But one of you knew or I wouldn't be here. However, I'm sure the dream started with Fleur."

"Me? Dream? What dream? Of you crashing?"

"Of me flying. Of me up in the wild blue yonder. Of you up in the wild blue yonder."

"I don't know how to respond to that. Your plane was repaired. You survived. Haven and I have both flown with you."

"Hmm. I wonder who magically repaired my plane? I wonder who made sure I survived? Was that in your heart?"

"I ... I don't know ... I wished the plane would fly again, I wished we'd find you alive ..."

"You've both flown with me. And here we've landed on an island you or I knew nothing about but which concealed the treasure Haven wanted. Tell me something, Fleur. Did you ever want to fly? Did you ever want to control the aircraft?"

Fleur stared at Amelia. "I did."

"But?" Amelia prodded.

"Haven said it wasn't important to the story. That I'd spoil the plot and subvert our characters."

"Subvert? Subvert whose character? Since when does freedom to fly subvert anyone? It certainly doesn't subvert birds or angels."

"Well, I'm neither of those, am I?"

"This is a whimsical novel we're in, isn't it? And Haven is no longer around to overwrite your passions or prayers, is she? So, let's find out who you are and what you are. Climb on board. Get in the pilot's seat."

"I ... I don't know anything about planes, Amelia."

"But I do. I'll guide your hands. Open up your mind. Take you to the sky. The plane is fully fueled, Fleur. Get behind the controls. Let's go find where you are in all those vast stretches of clouds and sapphire and sunlight."

Chapter 28 — Season of Fire

I actually thought I'd hear about Luna getting engaged to Mark before I'd hear about Eve getting engaged to James. But as another hurricane missed us and roared out to sea in early October, giving us the back of her hand, the news came with Kara. A part of me had never expected to hear it from Eve herself, but another part definitely had hoped that if she fell in love with James, she'd talk to me about it like old times. But there were no old times anymore. I should not have set myself up for them.

Kara didn't even want to tell me. But she took me out for coffee and said there was no way I should hear about this along with the other waves and flotsam of island gossip. Eve had told her when they'd met on the street, showing off her diamond, and Kara had texted me and tugged me into Inked sixty minutes later. I didn't want to cry but I did a little bit. Only a little bit. Kara handed me a Puff from her jeans pocket.

"I did try to talk to her," Kara said as I wiped my eyes.

"About what?" I asked.

"About you. About her. We went to Breakers for over half an hour."

"And?"

"And ... she said she prayed for you every day. Cared for you very deeply. But."

"But?"

"She wasn't willing to sacrifice her relationship with Luna or James. Or Mark for that matter. Luna remains dead set against you, and James and Mark support her in that. So, Eve feels she has no choice. Especially since she's set to marry James this fall."

I blew my nose. "Okay. No choice. Got it."

"Eve did confess a couple of things."

"Confess?"

Kara shrugged. "For one, she doesn't get Luna's hostility. It seems over the top to her. She thinks there has to be a past on that. But Luna never talks about it, never talks about her animosity towards you. Eve says it's worth your life to try and bring Denna Patrick up around Luna."

"Oh, yes, for sure, I'm well aware of what a threat I am to another humans, especially women."

"Other women don't feel that way. None of our crew have ever felt that way—Jazz, Issime, Lincoln, Kaz. This is a Luna Marshall original."

"You said there were a couple of things?"

"Yeah. Eve said she didn't know how to read Mark."

"About what?"

"About Luna. About you. Sometimes, he's literally hanging off Luna. Other times, he's a million galaxies away."

This said nothing to me. "So? His mind is always all over the universe—wondering, dreaming, writing, taking everything in."

"Eve gets the feeling Mark finds Luna too ... light."

"That doesn't make any sense to me."

Kara bit her thumbnail which she did now and then when she was trying to figure something out. "It's been several months, right? Since they've been together? I mean, they were together how long before Mark showed up with her in June? I'm saying half a year now, six months—they've been connected for at least six months. You obviously get to know a lot about a person in that amount of time. Especially with all the days they spend together here. Like, every day pretty much. So, Eve thinks he's waiting and watching for something more … umm … profound to come out of her mouth. Something heavyweight. Or out of her keyboard."

"She's guessing. What does it matter anyways? It has nothing to do with me. Neither of them have anything to do with me."

"Eve was in the kitchen at Mark's place when Mark randomly remarked you had written a poem in one of your blogs about seashells and how meaningful it was. This had something to do with Luna going on about trying to say something new and heavy duty about sea stars and conches and shorelines. About how difficult it was to be original about things connected to the ocean and to islands. He even quoted part of your poem. So, obviously he'd memorized it. You know, thinking it over, you have to wonder what the heck Mark was doing. How did he expect Luna to react when she's been so fragile when it comes to you? Either he was being the absent-minded professor type, or he was well aware of what he was doing and trying to provoke Luna."

"Or he was testing the waters to see if he could bring up a forbidden topic now that so much water has passed under the bridge."

"Who knows? Anyway, Luna exploded. And kept exploding a long time. Eve said Mark finally left the house, his house, right? And disappeared somewhere. She saw him through the window stuffing his pipe and taking long strides. Definitely not in stroll mode. He never returned before Eve and Luna made their way back to The Bristol for the night."

"And the next day?" I wanted to know.

"Back to normal," Kara replied. "Hey, honey, hey, darling. Nothing had happened. Swept under the rug."

I was actually able to smile. "That's an archaic expression for a twenty something."

Kara smiled back. We were both smiling for the first time in our conversation. "Archaic? I picked it up from my nana."

"So, what's the point of all this Mark talk?" I asked her.

"Point?" She bit her thumbnail again. "No point. Except."

"Except what? Do you know you have this habit of kind of dangling things out there and not resolving them?"

"Except. And this is coming from Eve, not me. She thinks Mark still has feelings for you."

"Really. But you don't?"

"Well, I don't hang out with Mark. Eve does. But okay from what she's said, yesss."

"Yes?"

"Yesss with all the extra s."

"This is coming from you?" I asked.

She grinned. "It's coming from me and Eve. Definitely."

I shook my head. This analysis made me feel like I'd had too much cold water too fast. "I have to say. It doesn't move me much."

"It doesn't?"

"Why should it?"

"Because."

"There you go again. Because? Just because he remembered a scrap of one of my poems I can't even bring to mind?"

"He did it knowing it would make his girlfriend react in the negative. In the extreme negative. Why would a guy who loved his girl do that?"

"We humans are complicated and conflicted. Right?"

"Yes, okay, we are, but it still makes no sense to me unless ..."

"Kara."

"Yeah, yeah. It makes no sense unless he's pushing back against her attitude because he's thinking of moving on."

"Moving on to who?"

"Quit acting like a Boy Scout."

"If you mean moving on back to me," I responded, "I think you're wrong. He dropped me like a rock and jumped into Luna's arms."

"Umm." Thumbnail bite. "Who dropped who? You're the one that wouldn't take the risk and go for R for Romance with Mark, you do remember that, right?"

I blew out a lot of pent up air that was loaded with emotions. "Yes yes yes. I remember that. I basically gave him away, and Luna scooped him up, is that what you're driving at?"

"Something like that."

"But when Luna blew up at me and threw me out of her life, he was quick to support her."

"Well, she was his girlfriend, Denna. Not you. And. Neither of us have any idea how he felt about her blow up at you in real time anyway. We have no idea if he tried to argue her out of her hard heart or how many times he might have brought it up."

"I guess not."

"For all we know it's an ongoing sore point with him or a source of ongoing tension between the two of them."

I laughed the short laugh I use when I don't feel like laughing but still go ahead. "You sound like a psychology book."

"Sometimes, I feel like a psychology book. All the girls are in relationships with guys right now except me. Yet I'm the one they come to for advice. "Love and Dating and Breakups" by Kara Wingate, MD."

"It's nice you've made it through med school."

"Isn't it?"

"And are certified as a clinical psychologist with the State of Massachusetts."

"Yep. All my hard work paid off."

"So," I said, "in case Mark Hawthorne comes to you for counseling, because you never know on this island, you can pass on a message from me."

"Which is?" Kara asked.

"I'm absolutely not interested. I'll never be interested again."

"And you did use the word *absolutely*."

"I absolutely did."

Denna's Blog

It's the season of fire

The leaves are all on fire

Each one is flame—a flame

Burning out of control

Every tree is a wick

Except for the fir and spruce and pine

Who are green and in love forever

Never lost in autumn's endings of endings

But the brown leaves

Fallen to our feet

Died in north winds and frosts

Passions exhausted

And no spring

No spring will ever come

I joined the girls for a three-day color tour of New England. Maine, New Hampshire, Vermont, Rhode Island, and we even crossed the border into New Brunswick. Lots of hikes and shopping and great food at—can I use the word, charming?—charming rustic hotels. One was built entirely of large peeled logs. Groaners. Ha ha. The place was way better than its offbeat name. Their restaurant had the best clam chowder and the best lobster bisque.

Every day was a blaze of golds and crimsons, of ambers and pumpkin orange. We stopped at Bean's in Freeport, Maine, and I picked up winter jackets and winter boots, all of it waterproofed against our wet snow and sleet. I roomed with Jazz and you know, we never talked over any of the hard stuff going on in our lives. We goofed around, me the twenty-nine and her the twenty-one or two, and the craziness did my heart and soul good.

Another near miss from a tropical storm stripped St. Silvan's of its final leaves. They were the island's flooring now, Lincoln said. I felt free inside myself to return to all my old haunts, bright leaves and brown leaves underfoot. White Shell, Rattling Stones Beach, Northwest ... I felt comfortable again at them all. Why? Because talking about Mark made me realize I didn't care about him anymore, and I certainly didn't need him in my life, or in my novels, or poems, or daydreams or prayers. I didn't need Eve or Luna either. My young island friends were more than enough. And the artists group? Well, I refused to let them put me over a barrel on that, there's an old framing expression. I showed up, sat, participated, read from my ongoing works: *She's Not Here, The Next Treasure Island* and, surprising myself, *Harvest*, the novel about the Amish me, Becca, which I thought I'd set aside forever and a day. I got good feedback from the group, some favoring the whimsy of *Treasure Island*, some the realism of *Not Here*, some the Amish fiction of *Harvest*, everyone offering suggestions, most of them very good and helpful suggestions.

Mark Hawthorne? He gave decent feedback too though we both, by unspoken common consent it seemed, limited our eye contact. He liked *Not Here* the most, said it reminded him of my ancestor novelist, SG Greenwood, who he was spending the fall reading. He said that, knowing I'm sure, that he was the male protagonist in the first draft, though I'd gone in and altered his name to Matthew Cuthbert before my first reading to the group. So, that was all civil enough, I'd expected no less from him, really, but when we took lunch at Breakers, I sat with Sydney Ryder and Scott Munro.

So, life was as good and clean as the Atlantic air and I thrived in it.

Then came November and the wedding.

Chapter 29 – Goodbye

I grew sentimental about things I shouldn't have been sentimental about. Just because of Eve's marriage. I thought back to my own wedding day, how kind Jacob had been that morning and the many mornings after. How we had both eaten an apple together our first day as a married couple, he taking a bite and then me taking a bite. How strong and warm his hand had been in mine when we walked a wooded path together, far away from the eyes of others. How sweet his few kisses had been––he'd always been shy about kisses.

Oh, such bizarre thoughts to indulge in. Talk about Amish fiction with extra-large rose-colored glasses on. Whatever romance we had was gone less than a year later. After that, our marriage was drudgery and laced with pain. Pain at not being able to have more children after Daniel. Pain at Jacob treating me like an enemy. Pain at him seeing me as an obstacle to the life and happiness and holiness he longed for with a house full of shining daughters and sons.

The ceremony took place on board *Nine Dolphins*. James received permission to tie up at the main wharf for two hours to make it easier for wedding guests to come on board or, when capacity on the boat was reached, to stand on the dock and watch. I saw it all from above, sitting on the glassed-in balcony of Kara's condo. She had invited me to join her and the girls who were free, not knowing, she told me, if I wanted to be anywhere near the wedding event. I actually didn't even want to be on the same island as the wedding event and had plans to take the early ferry to Boston. But prayer and an early morning walk softened my heart and I showed up at Kara's door. Issime and Jazz were there too. We could look right down at the harbor front and onto the deck of the sailing boat.

There was still enough Amishness in Eve to want a November wedding. November was the traditional month--the harvest was done, the farming finished for the year. Though it's true some Amish churches have begun to hold spring weddings just before or just after spring planting, most still adhere to the month of November. But that was about the only thing Amish that Eve had apparently insisted on.

When Eve showed up in a silver limo, she stepped out wearing a pretty stunning white dress with a train that needed two flower girls to keep under control. She did the whole thing--glittering gown, head piece and veil, white stilettos. James was in a white tux. Mark was in a white tux too and was best man as well as the minister officiating. There were flowers everywhere ... in the rigging, scattered on the deck, in Eve's arms as well as twined in her crown-braided silvery hair. James had put up colorful signal flags, the brass had been polished till the sunlight bounced off, the hull scrubbed so it became a mirror to the water. I was taken in by it all, I have to admit.

I was even able to handle super slender Luna in an aquamarine dress with sequins that sparkled and flashed every time she moved. She stood and posed, all smiles, as Eve's maid of honor.

I was able to handle her until the reception on board the ship, that is. Once she was glomming onto Mark, wine glass in hand, grinning up into his rugged, tanned and handsome sea captain face--he'd grown a very nice dark beard he kept perfectly trimmed-- that about used up all the grace God had given me for the day. I said *adios* to the girls, told them I needed a time out and took off half-running, half-walking, making my way past the harbor and onto the beach beyond, Northwest, and going nonstop until I came to Mark's Rock, which I hadn't intended to do. At least, I thought I hadn't intended to do that. I didn't intend to stay there and sit by it either. But I did that too.

Eve had wound up with a spectacular fall day. Warm, hardly any sea breeze, cloudless. I watched the mainland for a while but mostly I didn't want to watch anything except the face of God. I leaned my head against the rock and stared up at the blue. God, what Kara called the Universe but I didn't, poured a fresh stream of grace into me. How else do you explain my ability to not only pray for Eve's marriage but to pray for Mark's relationship with Luna? And want good for Luna and Mark? Ask for blessing upon blessing for them till I'd asked for so many blessings I felt free of most of my hurt, and resentment, and my sense of loss and rejection. I had refused to admit those cuts existed in my heart before the wedding. Now it was ridiculous to say I wasn't bleeding. But

I'm not just saying the prayers helped so I can sound so spiritual and so far above all the agony. I'm just stating facts. The longer I did this kind of praying, the more a feeling of wholeness came over me. Like a soft rain that brought no chill with it but which washed me clean.

I saw no reason to move. A lot was happening inside my head and heart. Thinking and praying and all kinds of healing were going on at the same time. I had fled the pain in Pennsylvania and found a measure of relief on St. Silvan's. But now pain from a different source had found me here too. Part of it had followed me from Pennsylvania (Eve) and part of it had been waiting for me here in the guise of a fellow author (Mark). Another part of it had pounced by means of that author's girlfriend and student (Luna). I hadn't seen any of it coming. How could I? It had struck deep and fast.

Yet now, I had gentle words inside myself and gentle warmths I could not explain unless I brought God into the picture: *I won't leave you. I cannot. I won't abandon you. I will not.* God's face was so human, so strong, so brave, so kind, so bracing. The love was inescapable. I'd brought sour thoughts about him to Massachusetts Bay. My entire first year on the Atlantic had been a kind of wrestling match, except I was Jacob in the Bible story, not the Jacob everyone expected. I had no idea if I'd prevailed in any way at all or if I'd earned a new name. But the past few weeks, I'd been set alight like a candle, and there was no question that darkness had not prevailed over me. Even the sword thrust of the wedding, and seeing Luna with Mark where I had not been invited and could not be, had not wounded me enough to be fatal to my heart and soul. Here at Mark's Rock, of all places, angels had found me, and the God they served, he had found me too and lingered.

I knew James had plans to sail down the coastline to Florida and into the Caribbean so long as no storms were in the offing. What I didn't know was a second wedding ceremony was planned for Pennsylvania. The party of four, James and Eve, Luna and Mark, flew out from Boston and stayed with Eve's family for a few days. The clothing for the Pennsylvania wedding was more restrained, the ceremony more religious and subdued. Not Amish because James was not Amish and Eve wasn't much of an Amish woman anymore either. But respectable enough that Eve's parents and the rest of the church could accept it and attend and bless the couple. I heard all this from Kara who heard it from Eve when the four returned to St. Silvan's to board *Nine Dolphins* for the cruise south. And Eve had asked Kara to tell me. That's what Kara said anyway.

I was actually at the Kennedys when they rounded the point and headed for Florida, hugging the shoreline as close as they dared. I wasn't at the cliffs by accident or coincidence. I counted on them taking that route. Why I felt I had to see them off, I have no idea. I knew it didn't matter to them. I didn't think it should matter to me. But as the sun broke clear of the sea they came in sight, turned to gold a moment or two, passed under my feet and sped away on the wind. I wished them well, I prayed them well.

Eve, James, Luna, Mark. I blessed them. That's the word for it. I even raised my hand as they swept by. Goodbye. God bless you. Goodbye, Mark. Goodbye.

Chapter 30—So Long as Men Can See or Eyes Can Breathe

BECCA: I DON'T KNOW WHAT TO SAY.

ME: WHY SAY ANYTHING THEN?

BECCA: YOU DON'T THINK IT'S GOOD TO TALK?

ME: NOT WHEN EVERYTHING'S BEEN TALKED TO DEATH. PRAYED TO DEATH. HOPED TO DEATH. LISTEN, I FEEL STRONG, OKAY? I FEEL CLOSE TO GOD. I FEEL CLOSE TO ME. I FEEL CLOSE TO JOY. WHAT IS THE POINT OF REHASHING EVERYTHING CHAPTER AFTER CHAPTER? EVE, LUNA, MARK. IT DOESN'T MATTER ANYMORE. I DON'T NEED ANY OF THEM TO BE COMPLETE OR TO HAVE A FUTURE. OR TO HAVE GOD AND A SOUL, FOR THAT MATTER.

BECCA: FLYING THE AIRPLANE WON'T MAKE ANY DIFFERENCE. IT'S CLICHÉ.

ME: MAYBE. BUT I'VE NEVER FLOWN A PLANE. I NEVER WILL FLY A PLANE. SO, IT'S A NICE METAPHOR TO EMPLOY. A CRASHED PLANE. A REPAIRED PLANE. A PLANE FLYING AGAIN. ME AT THE CONTROLS. I'M PUTTING FLOATS ON THE PLANE AS WELL. I WANT TO LAND AT ISLANDS ALL OVER THE WORLD AND JUST FLOAT ON THE SEA.

BECCA: SOUNDS LIKE YOU HAVE NO HOME THEN.

ME: FREEDOM IS MY HOME.

BECCA: *JA?* FREEDOM IS YOUR HOME? THAT SOUNDS *SCHMALTZY.*

ME: I DON'T CARE IF IT SOUNDS LIKE *SCHMALTZ* OR *SCHNAPPS.* THAT'S WHERE I WANT TO BE. PHYSICALLY FREE, EMOTIONALLY FREE, SPIRITUALLY FREE. REMEMBER THAT PART OF THE BIBLE? THE TRUTH SHALL SET YOU FREE? *JA?* THAT'S WHERE I AM. NOTING CORNY ABOUT THAT. UNLESS A FAITH IN GOD THAT GIVES A PERSON A FULL AND RICH LIFE, AND BRINGS THAT PERSON OUT OF SUFFERING, IS SOMETHING CORNY TO YOU.

BECCA: WHERE IS THIS ALL GOING TO END UP?

ME: GOD KNOWS. I DON'T. REALLY. I DON'T KNOW THAT PART OF MY STORY YET.

BECCA: EXCEPT YOUR PLANE CAN FLOAT NOW.

ME: YES. AND I CAN FLOAT TOO.

With December, and the lights and decorations going up in the harbor and downtown, I began to set my own life in order. When I would do my blogs. When I would work on my books, not just the fanciful ones, but the one that mattered the most to me, *I'm Not Here.* Making sure my walks were never missed. Making sure I got up to the lighthouse deck several times a week (Kara had slipped me a key so I could use the inside staircase, ensuring my climbs were infinitely easier, and I wouldn't "lose my grip on the ice and break my crazy X-Amish neck.") Prayer? I had my prayer here, there and everywhere (a

Dr. Seuss prayer pattern). And swimming? I still did my Iceberg Swimming. It definitely jolted me enough to keep me alive.

Though being alive wasn't a problem. My life was like looking out to sea towards England and Ireland and France on a good day. Or even on a stormy day. Lots of space. Maybe clouds, maybe not. A vast horizon that blended water to sky in grays or blues or both. Wind. Gulls. Sandpipers. Surf that erased tracks and made sand beaches smooth and rock beaches rattle. The burst of breakers. The fires of whitecaps. The cries of the birds and the breaking open of ocean on rocks and shore. Maybe the sea flat and shining as polished metal. Maybe the sea a scramble of currents, crosscurrents and power. Maybe a thousand miles of calm. Maybe a thousand miles of restless energy and shifting tides. Maybe something brought to my feet from a thousand fathoms deep. My life was sweet and spilling over the sides of my glass, a glass that was always full even if others couldn't see it.

Denna's Blog

There's not much that can be written about the sea that hasn't been written over and over again for thousands of years. Still, that doesn't mean we stop. We just find new ways of saying it. We use different words, different metaphors, we become more poetic than we usually are. Instead of waves breaking, waves split. Instead of wind blowing, wind cuts. Instead of sun shining, the sun is burning. Instead of stars bright over the sea at night, stars are light and the sea has no night. I think talking about the ocean and its beauty and mystery is like talking about the beauty and mystery of God––for all that's been spoken and written, the subject is inexhaustible, the metaphors and points of view we can employ, unlimited.

Was it the right thing or a mistake to return to beaches I'd walked with Mark and attempt to reclaim them? I thought about this a long time and then said, hey, whose beaches are they anyway? Who do they belong to? Why are they lost to me forever? Mark doesn't own them. The past doesn't own them. Good memories that have become bad memories don't own them. They don't have to be prison camps. I can set them free. They can set me free, even more free than I already am. So, I went back to all the beaches and made them part of my weekly routine, snow or sleet or ice blue winter calm. It was not so bad. A twinge here, a stab there, but not so bad.

I'd been back to Northwest once before. On the day of Eve's wedding. I'd even gone to Mark's Rock. He hadn't named it that. I had. Back in the day when it was wreathed in seaweed and pipe smoke. Now I came to it again. I was even free enough to quote Shakespeare to myself. It was a little sad, okay, definitely sad. But at the same time, it was all right. Shakespeare suited the shore. Suited looking across at Gloucester. *But thy eternal summer shall not fade, nor lose possession of that fair thou ow'st.*

I decided to speak the next lines out loud as if I were on stage.

"Nor shall death brag thou wander'st in his shade!
When in eternal lines to time thou grow'st!"

I was interrupted.

"So long as men can breathe or eyes can see
So long lives this, and this gives life to thee."

I did not want to be interrupted in my own little healing ritual.

Especially not by him.

"What are you doing here?" I snapped.

Mark stood there in jeans, and boots, and a denim shirt and navy pea coat. Gloucester was behind him. "I was walking."

"No, you weren't. You're in the Caribbean."

"Our eyes can play tricks."

"I don't want you here."

"Nevertheless."

"I'm doing fine without you. More than fine. Go away. Leave me alone."

"I will. But first I need to say something."

I glared fire. "You need to say something? There's nothing you need to say that I need to hear."

"A moment."

"No. No, no, no."

"I'm sorry, Denna. I'm so sorry I hurt you. That we all hurt you."

I wanted to run. I didn't but I came close. The only reason I didn't run was because I was too proud. Why should I run from him?

"You wouldn't know," he said, standing there in his sea captain beard and peacoat, "how many fights I had with Luna over you."

"I don't care!" I spat.

I felt like pelting him with stones.

"Right from the very beginning, Denna. Right from the moment she snubbed you."

"Don't use my name!"

"I tried to reason with her. Tried to get her to alter her attitude."

"*Alter her attitude?* Who are you? Professor Alliteration? I don't care what you tried to do. So far as I'm concerned, you didn't do anything. Except hang off her arm."

"I got the impression," he went on in his calm voice, "that you wanted nothing to do with me when I left St. Silvan's for Salem. Once I returned with Luna, I was ecstatic when you two became fast friends. Prayers answered. I did not see her jealousy coming. I was as blindsided as you were."

"But you stayed with her. No matter how mean-spirited she got. No matter that she cut me out of the group and off the sailboat. No big deal, right? You supported her. You backed up everything she did that was cruel."

"I did not. I fought with her over everything she did. I warned her over and over again."

"Warned her about what?"

"That I would leave her."

"*Ja?* So, why didn't you?"

"First of all, I knew you wouldn't want me."

"Correct, Professor."

"Second of all, I held out hope I could persuade her to change her ways. To become friends with you again. To write that book with you. I truly thought there was a chance."

"Why? Why on earth would you think that?"

"Because ... sometimes she had a soft word for you ... sometimes she had a kind thought ... and I hoped ..."

"She did? Luna did?"

"She did, Denna."

"Don't say that. Don't use that word. Don't use my name."

No, I could not stop the tears. No, I could not stay in a rage even though I wanted to. I dropped down in the pebbles and sand facing Gloucester, swiping at my eyes with my fingers, my face wet. My whole body hurt.

"Everything was fine till you showed up," I moaned.

Chapter 31 – Mea Culpa

I wanted Mark to vanish.

Another part of me wanted him to keep talking.

So, I let him keep talking, as I stared across at Gloucester Harbor.

"I've been hoping to find you on one of our ... on one of the beaches for days," he explained. "I didn't come to argue or state my case. Not really. I came to apologize. I never agreed with anything Luna did when it came to you. I fought her at every point. It was a mistake to stay with her once I saw what she was capable of when it came to hurting and damaging another human being. It's not that I wanted Luna so much."

"What did you want then?"

"Friendship. Companionship. What I had with you."

"What you had with me. But wanted more. A more I didn't know if I wanted or not." I closed my eyes as a calm came over me, like a wind suddenly dropping and the ocean chop disappearing. "When did you leave the others?"

"A week ago. I took a flight into Boston. I stayed in Salem a couple of days before I returned to St. Silvan's. I've been wandering the beaches looking for you ever since."

"*He wandered the beaches looking for her, looking for hope, hoping for a friend.* I could write a poem. Why didn't you just come to my cottage?"

"No."

"No?"

"That was not the right setting."

"Why not?"

"Because … shorelines and sea wind and breakers and swooping gulls, that was always us. It was important I tell you how sorry I am, what a fool I've been, a fool all around."

I kept my eyes closed. "*A fool all around, a fool around town, a fool on the shore.* Another poem. A repentant Hawthorne has become my muse. But what do your words mean?"

"They mean …" He hesitated. "They mean I was wrong to walk away from you in the first place. So what if you weren't ready for a romantic relationship? Why should that have mattered? We still had our beach moments, our time at the church, our coffees, our quotes. I loved all of it. Why throw it away because you weren't in a place to say, '*Kiss me, you fool*?'"

I almost laughed but I refused myself. "That's a cliché thing to say."

"May I sit beside you?"

"No."

He remained standing. "It was pride on my part. Wounded pride. I took your struggle as a rejection. It wasn't a rejection. It was you trying to come to terms with your past, with your relationship with your dead husband, with what being intimate with another man might look like. What a lot of tough things to process. I was not considerate. Instead, I was impatient and moved on abruptly. Never called you from Salem. Never texted you. Proud and vain and obstinate. So yes, Denna, a fool all round."

"Leave my name out of it, please."

"All right."

"You don't have to *mea culpa* forever. Or maybe you do. I don't know what I want from you now. Nothing, I suppose. But I would not be honest to God if I didn't admit to my own part in all of this. I could have said something instead of just taking our friendship for granted. That you'd always be around even if it took me years to work through my junk. I was pretty casual and random about our relationship. Definitely, I wanted you to stay by my side. Definitely, I wanted to keep talking to you. Definitely, I wanted ... I wanted you to hold me in your arms like you did last Christmas. I felt so safe and sane and solid inside those arms. I should have said more.

"But now, I have nothing to say. Except I'm sorry that whole mess with Luna happened. I'm sorry it tore apart my friendship with you. I'm sorry you didn't come to me, cap in hand, months ago. Those are the only words I have. I don't want to be your friend again. In a remote way, okay, but I don't want to get close to you. I'm afraid you'll hurt me again. So, maybe we should just shake hands and you can be on your way."

"Can we talk more?"

I shook my head. "Not right now. This, what we've had here, it's enough. Perhaps we can have coffee tomorrow. I don't know. I don't know how I'll feel about you tomorrow. I don't know how I'll feel about us. But you can text me and we'll see. If you want. I don't know what sort of company I'll be. My faith tells me to forgive you. I've learned a lot about forgiveness on this island in two years, and yes, I know I can forgive you, I know I will forgive you. But I have no idea what I can do beyond that. I have no idea where I can go. If this were a novel, I could write in whatever I wanted. But you and I aren't in a novel, and to be honest, I don't know what I want so far as real life goes. Or I do know, but I don't want to say it. I have no desire to tell you. I have no desire to tell anyone. I don't even have a desire to tell God. Which is silly, of course, because he already knows. I'm so confused and conflicted I wouldn't trust anything I said out loud anyway. Text me in the morning. I'll tell you how I feel about coffee or how I don't feel."

"I understand," he replied.

Now I did give out a short laugh. "Do you? Because I don't understand anything at all."

Chapter 32 – Mark Hawthorne is Back

I'm Not Here

It was not as if they'd been lovers.

They'd never been lovers.

It had not been romance fiction.

Simply a beautiful friendship.

So, why was she acting as if they had been lovers? That they'd broken up and he'd left her for another woman?

Get serious, Denna, she told herself.

She and Mark had not been lovers. Not been engaged. Not been married. Had not even kissed. He had betrayed their friendship. He had stood with those who shunned her. It was a loss of friendship. Bad enough. But not a loss of love.

Unless.

Denna walked White Shell that night, The Night of Mark Hawthorne's Return, with only the cold and snowflakes that fell like winter stars for company. And waves that broke sharp along the shoreline. The sky overhead was clear. But nothing became as clear and open to her as the sky and its constellations. There was an "unless" in the air. It had never gone away. She didn't want to deal with it.

ME: I don't think the morning will work for coffee.
MARK: Okay. I'm sorry to hear that.
ME: Maybe another day. I'll text you.
MARK: All right, I understand.
ME: You do? Just like yesterday? You understand? I still don't understand anything.

Two days after Mark showed, Eve showed up.

I came in from a long walk, writing my daily blog in my head, opened the door (which I'd left unlocked) and there she was.

Sitting at the kitchen table in a white Patagonia fleece, black leggings and black snow boots. A Boston Red Sox ball cap on her head. A long silver ponytail hanging down the middle of her back. She arched her blonde eyebrows.

"You don't have peanut butter," she accused me. "Or celery."

I flopped down across from her, leaving my boots and jacket on too, even though the cottage was warm enough. "If only I'd known you were coming."

"Past time."

"Is it?"

"Yes. I'm sorry."

"You're sorry?"

"I'm sorry. James can tell you he's sorry himself."

"Did you all attend some kind or religious revival?"

Eve sighed and shook her head. Then she leaned back and stared up at the ceiling. "Sometimes it's like you've taken some kind of drug. Or inhaled a toxic vapor. And you act all weird, *ja?* You're oblivious to the way you're behaving. It doesn't seem out of the ordinary. Actually, you feel like you're as normal as normal can be. Even things that seem out of place, you're okay with. They're not that bad. Then one day, the haze clears. Like a mist burning off the ocean at sunrise. Suddenly there's clarity and color and high definition. Suddenly things can be distinguished one from the other. This is this and that is that, this isn't that and that isn't this. I don't know how it was with Mark, but that's how it was with me."

I shrugged. "He told me he fought with her from day one over the way she was treating me."

"He did. I'm witness to the clashes they had over you. It was ridiculous when I think back. He wanted you included in everything we did like you'd been included from the start."

"If he was that upset, why didn't he walk out?"

Eve brought her eyes down from the ceiling. "Didn't he tell you?"

"Tell me what?"

"He left her a week after we'd been in the Caribbean."

"A week? Where did he go?"

"Salem. That wasn't the first time. During the summer and fall, they must have broken up five or six times. Over you. He'd hang out in Salem for a few days, and then, they'd try to patch things up. It never lasted. He wouldn't tolerate her speaking a single word against you in his presence. And he kept delivering these ultimatums: *'If we don't start bringing Denna back into the loop I can't stay with you, Luna. Denna is my friend.'*"

"He did not say that." My head was in a swirl. "I don't believe you."

Translation: I don't want to believe you.

Advanced translation: I don't want to believe you because it will make my life less complicated if I don't.

Extreme translation: I may be wrong.

Eve placed her hand over her heart. "James can corroborate me. Even Luna, if she's in a mood to fling the truth in your face."

"Then why ... why didn't he come back to me in August or September?"

Eve arched her platinum eyebrows again. "Come back to you? Were you in a relationship that he should come back to you?"

"He could ... he might have ... stopped by as an old friend and ... explained what was going on ..."

She shook her head. "No. He was ashamed, that's part of it, ashamed of how we'd turned our backs on you. But the bigger truth? He was convinced you didn't like him all that much. Right from the time you sort of drifted out of his life here on the island. I'm not saying that's a good excuse. Definitely it's how he felt though. I heard him tell James all of this more than once. Why would Denna want to see him? Why would she be interested? *One day I'll apologize and walk out of her life for good. I'm not ready to take that walk yet.* That was Mark. Yes, he made a hash of everything. A *Schlamassel*. But—and this is something James and I have discussed—clearly the guy is—he's caught up in you."

I stared at her. "He's caught up in me. Really. And this is how he showed it? A shunning?"

"Luna is strong-willed. For too long, the rest of us were not. We did not try to resist. Except Mark. From the beginning, he fought back. No, he didn't come to you. But he certainly fought for you. He told us he saw you earlier this week. He's not sure you will want to see him again. *I don't blame her.*"

I looked over her shoulder at the window. It was snowing again.

"Did you sail back?" I asked.

"At this time of year? We flew. James and I will go back down after Christmas."

"What about Luna?"

"When we had the big split of all four of us, she went to see her sister in Texas."

"Texas. Do you think she'll be back?"

"Who knows. But Mark Hawthorne is back."

"What does that mean?" I put my hands over my eyes, elbows on the table. "*Mark Hawthorne is back.* I have no idea what that means."

Chapter 33—Sonnet 18

I decided to take a big risk.

Unusual for me.

You might respond: *Denna, you left Pennsylvania. All on your own. Started a new life. That was a risk.*

I suppose. But that was a risk I was confident (or fairly confident) I could handle. This new risk, I wasn't confident I could handle at all. Yet I felt I needed to take it or die. Which sounds very dramatic. I know that. But it was very dramatic.

I put aside Becca and *Harvest* where she was telling me it was time to come home and be her.

I put aside Fleur and Amelia and *The Next Treasure Island*. I left them bobbing on their float plane at the literal edge of the world where the seas ran over the side of the earth into space like the mightiest Niagara Falls ever created. They were asleep as the sun dropped over the edge of the falls and lit them up like twin fires.

I put aside *I'm Not Here*. Denna was walking a shoreline. Denna was always walking a shoreline. I couldn't be in third person anymore. I needed to be right here. Right now.

ME: Are you free?

HE: Yes.

ME: Meet me?

HE: Where?

ME: At your rock. At our beach. Can you do that? Is that okay?

HE: Of course, I can do that.

ME: Do you ... do you want to do that?

HE: I very much want to do that. The bigger question is: Do you want to do that? Can you even forgive me?

ME: I've already forgiven you. This is about going beyond forgiveness.

HE: Going beyond forgiveness? What does going beyond forgiveness mean?

ME: No more texting. We can't do this by texting. Northwest. Half an hour.

I got up on the rock and watched him approach.

Sea Captain Hawthorne with his beard and his peacoat and his pipe in hand.

It was a cold, crisp, windless *Blue Sky, Blue Water Day*. A novel co-authored by Lyyndenna Patrick and SG Greenwood.

I held up my hand the moment he reached me.

"I've been wrestling with the hardest thing I've wrestled with," I told him. "Okay. Maybe the third hardest thing. I have no idea where to go with it. I don't even want to tell you about it. Because I have no idea where you will go with it. But there is a reason what you did hurt so much."

"I know there's a reason," he responded. "I failed you. I failed our friendship."

"Let me finish. I know how you defended me against Luna's attacks and how you argued for me to be brought back into the group. That has been some balm to my wounds. You should have told me yourself. But finding out now is better than never. And you should have come to me sooner. But you've come to me now and that's enough to work with."

"What are we working with?"

"Us. You and me. Ourselves."

"What?"

"It was a lot more than wounded pride or wounded friendship that crushed me this past summer. I reacted strongly, so strongly, to what cut so deeply. I didn't just get hurt by the loss of a friendship. Yes, that was very painful. But I was reacting to something else I could not admit to myself. I was reacting to the loss of a love. I realize that, Mark. It hurt so much because you broke my heart. I love you."

I felt dizzy letting it out, letting out something I'd held in for so long. I felt crazy. But I knew it was true. It had taken me a long time to get there. But I knew it was there.

Mark looked as if he'd faint.

His face was like snow.

"What?" He stared at me. "I thought you'd hate me."

"I don't hate you. I can't even begin to hate you. I want to go somewhere with you. We have healing to work on. We have trust to work on. We have shorelines to work on. But I don't even know if you want to do that kind of work. I don't even know if you want to go somewhere with me. Do you? Do you, Mark?"

I had no idea how he'd respond. I really didn't. Everything had been so messy and it was still messy. But I wanted to try. I really wanted to try. I so hoped he wanted to try with me.

He thrust his hands into the pockets of his peacoat.

"Denna," he said. Then stopped. "Can I say Denna?"

I nodded. "Yes. I want you to use Denna now if you're going to say ... going to say something that belongs in romance fiction."

"I think we might have a fit."

"Then tell me. Say something. Can we heal together? Walk together? Watch the sea roll and break together? What? What can we do, Mark?"

"There was never a time I wasn't in love with you."

Now it was me. "What?"

"There wasn't. There simply wasn't. I just had to hold it in. All this time. For fear you'd run. Leave the island. Take yourself far away from me. Shut me out. I didn't know what to do about you. I've never known what to do about you."

The right word is staggered. I was staggered.

"But I love you, Denna. I love you so much. I just don't know how to go forward from where we find ourselves right now."

I jumped off the rock.

His arms were around me. *Thank you, God.* I closed my eyes and took in the rich scent of pipe tobacco that lingered on his coat. I thought of warm fires, tall ships, high white waves and the peace of a quiet harbor. I knotted my fingers in the denim shirt he wore.

"We'll find out," I said. "We'll take our time. Do every sunrise and sunset. Sit out under every full moon and every new moon dark and on fire with stars. Pray. Laugh. Whisper. Listen to God talking to you and me. We'll figure it out, Mark Hawthorne." I touched his lips with my fingers. *"So long as men can breathe or eyes can see, so long lives this and this gives life to thee."*

END

About the Author

Murray has released over two dozen fiction and nonfiction titles and been published with Elk Lake, HarperCollins, Harvest House, Baker, Barbour, MillerWords and Harlequin. His favorite genres include historical fiction and contemporary fiction. He makes his home in southwestern Alberta near the Waterton-Glacier International Peace Park.